The Hauntings of Playing God

Chris Dietzel

Published in the United States by CreateSpace Independent Publishing.

ISBN-13: 978-1500548261

ISBN-10: 150054826X

Cover Design: Truenotdreams Design

Author Photo: Jodie McFadden

ALSO BY CHRIS DIETZEL

<u>Apocalyptic</u>
The Man Who Watched The World End
A Different Alchemy
The Last Teacher

<u>Dystopian</u>
The Theta Timeline
The Theta Prophecy
The Theta Patient

The Hauntings of Playing God

1

Morgan's mother once said that a life starts the first time you tell another person you love them. That same life ends, she had said, no matter when your heart actually stops beating, the last time you make an announcement of love. Her mother was, obviously, a romantic at heart. But what about people that never find love? Surely, they are still alive. Aren't they?

Her father, much more practical, said life starts with your first heartbeat and ends with your last heartbeat. Too smart for her own good, even as a little girl, Morgan had immediately replied, "What if someone gets a heart transplant? Are they the person who's still alive, or is it the person that the heart originally belonged to?" Morgan's father did not bother with a response.

Her mother used to roll her eyes at these literal types of answers offered by her husband. Any time Morgan's father said life started with a breath of oxygen or with brain activity, Morgan's mother would pat her on the head and say you only truly lived as long as you were curious: life started the first time you asked 'Why?' and ended when you stopped asking such questions.

"If you keep telling her things like that," Morgan's father would say, giving a deep sigh, "she's going to grow up to be a hippie. Or worse, a journalist."

Little did Morgan's father know that journalists would be one of the many extinct vocations after the second decade of the Great De-evolution. With the end of man signaled, no one was interested in reading the same daily reports of human misery and tragedy they had been seeing for the previous hundred years. There were better ways to spend your time than hearing about corruption, needless death, and celebrity scandals.

Instead, people finally took time to start the books they had always wanted to read, spent time learning the hobby that had always interested them, or else they had actual conversations with the people they were sitting next to rather than watching the TV in silence. In those days, even though the world seemed to be going to hell, a lot of people would say their lives were more fulfilling after the Great De-evolution began than before it started.

One day, during her sophomore year of high school, a teacher—who she still isn't sure to this day if he was a good teacher or an awful one—asked the class if life ever really began or ended. He smirked and asked if life might be endless. Given that there were no freshman and she was part of the final graduating class, this seemed unlikely. Or, he offered a spooky face, is it all a figment of God's imagination. Maybe, he suggested, none of his students were actually there in his classroom, none of them were even alive, because they were part of a higher being's dream. The class stared back at him in silence; none of the teenagers knowing what to make of these comments. Maybe, if there had been more than three other students in class with her, someone would have raised their hand and offered a smart-ass reply. Being that they were in a room meant for twenty-five kids and only four desks were occupied, the kids all remained silent.

Following high school, one of the boys she dated said life began for men when they got their first erection and ended when they could no longer get it up. The boy smirked as he said it, as if that was her cue to start making out with him. It wasn't even sexist, it was just asinine. (There was no second date.) Was she to assume her life didn't start until she got her first period and ended when she was in her fifties? It was proof that people didn't stop saying stupid things just because the world's population was getting a little smaller each day.

Did her life start after her first breath? Maybe she truly began living once she understood that two people were looking down at her in her bed, ensuring she was safe and healthy. Or did her life start the first time she smiled? Did her life actually begin later, when she started asking her mother questions like, "Where do babies come from?" and "Will I have a little sister someday?"

She thinks of these possible benchmarks, takes stock of how many of these options indicate that her life is still progressing and by how many has it already ended.

She is still breathing. Check.

Her heart is still beating. Check.

It's been years since she has told someone that she loved them. Trouble.

And considering she is surrounded only by people who cannot talk or move, not by anyone who can love her, she does not see herself making the proclamation of love anytime soon. More trouble.

She has no idea if her high school teacher's comments about being part of a dream, about really existing, can ever be measured, so she strikes that out.

To this day, even at the age of ninety-three, she is still trying to figure out how she has arrived at this point, why she is one of two regular people left in the group home. Maybe her mother was right: maybe asking all of these "why" and "how" questions is keeping her alive.

None of the definitions she attempts to measure her own life with, save the ones about someone's first breath and their heartbeat, can apply to Blocks. No one knew what to do when babies all around the world were being born without the ability to move or speak or do anything at all, as if they were obstructed, or blocked, from the rest of the world. Not only were they born this way, they would remain motionless and mute the rest of their lives. It wasn't necessarily their appearance that signaled the end of humanity, it was the absolute disappearance of regular people who could create new, self-sustaining life. Now, except for Elaine, the only other caretaker working alongside Morgan, Blocks are the only people she knows.

But if the measure of breathing or of a heart beating is the only indication that Blocks are alive, does that really mean they are living? Does it mean that life is only about how long your lungs can take in new oxygen? Surely not. Deep down, in the set of core beliefs she has never shared with anyone else, she knows life is about more than just a heart beating or blood flowing. It has to be, or else there is no point to everything the human race has ever accomplished. Why mold steel, control electricity, conquer mountains, go into outer space, if all that matters is taking another breath of air?

What else is there, though? What else can there be? These are the questions that plague her. They follow her as she walks through the aisles of Blocks, caring for each one. The questions follow her to bed, no matter how exhausted her physical body is, and torment her dreams. They also greet her in the morning when she wakes up.

And the thoughts follow her now as she stands up, pushes her chair from under her, and turns around to face the Blocks whose health she is responsible for. She scans the many rows, each with a cross-aisle every twenty feet so she can easily move about, make her way in-between them.

Her desk and her computer are in the same over-sized room as her Blocks. The desk has probably been here since the building was first constructed, decades and decades earlier. The computer once belonged to a caretaker who arrived thirty years ago and has since passed away.

She has never been able to get over the guilt she feels the few times each week that she takes a couple of minutes away from caring for the bodies all around her so she can track the weather, e-mail the few other caretakers remaining around the world, or write in her diary. Having the rows of bodies behind her is a constant reminder she does not want. She feels their eyes on her back as she types an e-mail or looks at the weather reports for possible hurricanes. Their eyes pull her away from relaxation, force her to begin another round of chores.

"Relax," Elaine says when she sees Morgan stand up from the computer after only resting for five minutes. "I can handle it."

But Morgan doesn't sit back down. It's not possible when others rely entirely on her. The reason she has never been able to come to terms with these brief reprieves is that every minute away from the rows of beds means sixty-four mouths that can't chew their own food, that require nutrient bags, are not getting the attention they need. It means sixty-four Block diapers filled with excrement need to be changed. Each body needs to be washed and, to prevent bedsores, repositioned. Without her, sixty-four people begin the process of dying. And in her guilty conscience, they start dying as soon as she turns her back to look at her computer. She knows this is an over-dramatic simplification; it's not as though each body begins starving to death as soon as she washes her own hands or puts food in her own mouth. And they certainly don't begin to die just because she stays in touch with someone from the Los Angeles group home or checks for another storm.

It does feel that way, though.

2

Morgan and Elaine weren't always alone. There was a time when they were but two of the many caretakers walking aisles at the final Miami group home. During her first years working at the home for Blocks, Morgan had been assigned a four-hour shift. Four easy hours. And she had only been responsible for one quadrant. Each quadrant consisted of four rows with four Blocks in each row. She only had to feed and clean sixteen people. Looking back, she didn't know those were the days she should have considered herself lucky.

As the population slowly shrank, as more and more caretakers passed away, as no new people entered the city who were willing to volunteer their time, she took on more responsibility. At first, her four-hour shift turned into an eight-hour shift, but still caring for a single quadrant. A while later, the caretakers each became responsible for thirty-two Blocks during their eight hours. Then thirty-two Blocks for a twelve-hour shift. She stopped keeping track of her time once there were only four caretakers left. After that, there were no longer enough people to keep a sustained schedule of duties, so each person worked until they simply couldn't work anymore and had to rest. Each person took care of as many Blocks as they could until they collapsed from fatigue.

"Four people can't take care of so many bodies,"

George, the last remaining male caretaker, had said. "It's just not possible."

The other three had just looked at him, not wanting to ask what he was getting at, not wanting to admit they might be thinking the same thing.

He added, "Maybe if we gently assist a couple quadrants into the next life, we can do a better job of caring for the rest of them."

It had been Morgan who had stepped forward, said she would care for all of them by herself if she had to, and then began walking the rows to do just that. Even as she refilled the first nutrient bag, she couldn't think of a better reason for her outburst or her devotion other than the knowing that if she were one of the people who needed care, she wouldn't want to be neglected or tossed aside so easily. She refused to look behind her to see if the other three caretakers would follow her lead. Eventually, Elaine and the others shrugged and joined her. The topic hadn't come up again.

So focused were they on caring for the Blocks at that point that they stopped caring for themselves. A woman who took over after Morgan went to sleep simply fell over dead one day. Then there were only three caretakers left. That was when George either decided he had been right all along or else experienced what Morgan and Elaine think must have been a nervous breakdown. He simply walked out into the empty city streets without saying goodbye and was never seen or heard from again.

"I didn't see that coming," Elaine had said.

Morgan didn't say anything. She was too busy trying to remember if there had been any signs that someone she had spent almost every waking hour with for the past five decades could turn on her like that. Had he said or done anything in the days leading up to his disappearance that would signal a nervous breakdown? She didn't think so. Was it his way of excusing himself from a situation he didn't agree with? More likely.

Then there were only two caretakers left.

Two caretakers for sixty-four Blocks.

But then, a month earlier, Elaine began showing the first signs of sickness. Before the Great De-evolution, the cold probably would have been treatable. A doctor would have prescribed some pills and Elaine would have been back to feeling her usual self. After all, before the Blocks appeared, people had been routinely living to be one hundred years old. Men on TV had announced the birthdays of all the new centurions each morning, welcoming them to the growing club. But as the population declined and medical experts faded away, the average life expectancy slowly started to decline as well. Now, there is no one to diagnose whether Elaine's fever is a symptom of something more serious or just a bug she needs to sleep off.

At first, she had woken up with a cough, was sluggish through the day, complained of being too hot. Morgan wasn't a doctor. She wasn't even a nurse. She just took care of people because no one else was around. That didn't make her qualified to diagnose her friend's sickness.

"Go to bed. Rest." That's all she could offer.

Two days later, Elaine was back on her feet, helping Morgan with the chores as best she could.

"I used to have the immune system of a lion," she said.

Morgan looked down at her wrinkly hands and arthritic knuckles before saying, as if shocked, "I guess we're not as young as we used to be."

The comment did the trick. Elaine has always loved vastly understated cynicism. She is predictable that way. She smiled and shuffled ahead to the next bed and to the Block residing there.

Elaine has been healthy since that last bout of sickness. Now, as they make their way through the rows of Blocks, rain falls steadily on the metal roof three stories above them. They have to speak louder to hear each other above the constant barrage of water pinging off metal. The group home was originally a high school gymnasium. That was before it was gutted and turned into a Survivor Bill facility that made food processors for everyone.

Sixty-four beds seems like a lot when you have to care for the bodies occupying each one, but it does little to make an old basketball court and the expanse of rafters above it feel like a cozy place to live. The gymnasium used to house hundreds of Blocks. Now, only a fraction of that number remains. In such a large room, with so little to fill it, the pitter-patter of the rain echoes throughout each corner of the home.

"I was never a fan of the rain," Elaine says. "Not even as a kid when my brother used to think it was fun to play baseball during storms like this. I'd watch him from the window and think he was crazy."

Morgan listens to the water droplets pounding away at the roof and closes her eyes. "I used to love lying on the ground when I was a kid and it was raining like this. The ground starts off really hard and dry, but after a couple of minutes you feel like you're sinking right into the earth."

"Morgan?"

"Yeah?"

"You have a lot of issues."

This is how Morgan knows Elaine is feeling better again.

3

It was Elaine's idea, back when she and Morgan became the final two caretakers, to begin naming each Block. Not only that, but to create a story for each Block's life, as if they were an additional normal person occupying the group home rather than a body needing daily care. Before that, they had just seemed like random bodies.

"Jimbo, here," Elaine would say from the bed she was standing over in quadrant 1, "was the cop who finally decoded the Block Slasher's letters and brought him to justice."

It was a source of amusement that made Morgan uncomfortable. She was reminded of dumb make-out games from middle school, like spin the bottle and seven minutes in heaven—games that even as a girl she had thought were a waste of time. Although she had gone along with them at more than one party.

She didn't say it, but her first thought was, *He doesn't look like a cop. He looks like a frail old man who's never moved from that bed or eaten a solid meal.*

"This one," she said instead, calling across the gym from the cot she was standing by in quadrant 3, "was—"

"This one?" Elaine said, unhappy with how the game was being played. "What's her name?"

"Cindy."

"Okay. What did Cindy do?"

Morgan tried to think of something a little more positive than a story involving the Great De-evolution's most notorious serial killer. "She, uh, she was a comedian."

Elaine gave a nod, as if that was what she had been thinking too.

The next day, as Elaine refilled Jimbo's nutrient bag, she yelled over to Morgan, "He had to shoot the Block Slasher five times. There was no way the killer would allow himself to be taken alive."

In response, Morgan said, "Cindy's whole act revolved around the Great De-evolution. Anyone who was sad about the human race dying out could go to one of her shows and, after a couple minutes of jokes, would think our extinction was the funniest thing in the world."

The next day, Elaine added, "Jimbo was only able to break the Block Slasher's code after reading a copy of one of Leonardo da Vinci's old notebooks. The Slasher was a huge fan of everything to do with the Renaissance."

Morgan dabbed Cindy's lips with a wet cloth to keep them from cracking. "Cindy was in the process of getting her own sitcom before the networks closed their doors. They had just gotten done filming the pilot for her show and then the whole network shut down."

"Life's a bitch," Elaine said, approving of the C-level celebrity in their midst.

Each Block was given a name and a story, and every time they walked the rows of beds, each story was developed a little more. Day after day went by with the two of them adding a bit here and a piece there to each life in the cots around them. Eventually, Morgan and Elaine could recite each person's entire biography. And in that way, random bodies became valued members of society.

The following week, Elaine had called over to Morgan: "Jimbo said we're lucky he's not still on the job. He's sure there's more than one killer lying somewhere in the cots around us."

She's not serious, is she? Morgan thought. *We're going to put words in their mouths now?*

But she gave in because it would ruin Elaine's day, and maybe every day they had spent creating these fictitious lives together, if she stopped playing along now. She knew there had to be a reason for Elaine to develop this game all of a sudden, to provide something in their lives that was missing, she just didn't know what it was.

"Cindy says you're not welcome at her comedy shows. She's trying to make people laugh, not kill themselves."

"Ha!" Elaine called out, satisfied.

To this day, they still add thoughts and words to each body. And with the stories, with the dialogues they created on behalf of the people that couldn't talk for themselves, Morgan finds herself thinking of each body around her as an actual person, rather than a shell of a person. Even when Elaine doesn't yell across the gym to add another detail to a Block's life or relay what the Block just said, Morgan finds herself thinking of the things each Block might say. She passes one, known for being gruff, and frowns at his comment that she should stand upright and have better posture. Then she passes a Block known for being happy-go-lucky, and smiles at the comment that the prettiest daylight always follows storm clouds.

Under her breath, she says, "Yes, that's true."

Maybe that is what Elaine intended the entire time, that they would start to think of themselves as part of a group again. Without her friend's game, Morgan could envision herself resenting the daily allotment of chores. When you are old and weak, it takes all the energy you have to care for others. If the rows of anonymous bodies she cleans and feeds could have been swapped out for any other collection of nameless bodies, she might become irritated with her situation. Giving each Block a unique life, giving them personalities, carrying on conversations with them, makes each body a special addition to the facility. Instead of being burdened by an assortment of mannequins she is surrounded by some of the world's most interesting people, people she just happens to be caring for.

"Cindy wants to know if you've heard the one about the Block, the priest, and the rabbi," she says.

But Elaine doesn't answer. Morgan sees her friend leaning over one of the Block's beds with her head down.

"Your forehead is on fire," she says when she gets there and puts a hand to Elaine's face. "You need to lie down."

The next day, Elaine seems healthy again. But the following week, she is ill for three days in a row. The next week, she is bedridden for all but one day.

"Is this what it's like to grow old?" Elaine says. "I'm tired of being sick."

"You'll be fine," Morgan says. "You're just pushing yourself too hard."

Even as she says it, though, her eyes dart all over the room. First, at all of the bodies waiting for care. Then at the computer and her one method of communicating with the outside world. Then at the emergency exit and the place she last saw George. Her eyes bounce all over the place, back and forth, like a terrified dog's, until Elaine squeezes her hand.

"What do you think Cindy has to say about me right now?" she asks.

But Morgan can't focus on the game. "You'll be fine," she says again. "You have to be."

Elaine looks around the room at all the people who are dependent on their care, then returns her eyes to gaze at Morgan. She opens her mouth to say something, but thinks better of it and only nods and closes her eyes.

"You'll be fine," Morgan says again.

Two days go by and Elaine seems to be slowly getting her strength back. But on the third evening, after Morgan gets done caring for the Blocks and eats her own dinner, she is shocked at what she finds. Elaine is mumbling in her sleep, but her eyes are open and worried, as if she doesn't understand where she is. Her breathing is raspy. Her face is covered in sweat. Tiny bits of perspiration collect on each part of her face until the droplets run down onto her pillow. Her white hair, which has significantly thinned over the years, is matted together with moisture.

Maybe, Morgan thinks, life is about the first time you tell yourself everything will be okay and the last time you are able to convince yourself of that lie.

In the morning, when Morgan opens her eyes, she notices Elaine is still under her blanket, still breathing as if afraid she might drown. Although she is asleep, she continues to shiver and mumble.

Morgan goes immediately to her side. "You're sick," she says, gently tugging on Elaine's shoulder. "Stay in bed. I'll take care of everything."

Elaine's eyes open, but they do not focus on Morgan or on anything else, and she does not offer a reply. Her eyes close again as the shivering continues uninterrupted.

Morgan has a quick breakfast and then begins her rounds. Halfway through, she goes to check on Elaine and sees she is no better. She finds a spare blanket and adds it to the other two already on top of her friend. The additional warmth does no good; the shivering does not stop or even become less pronounced.

It is almost midnight by the time she is done caring for all four quadrants of Blocks.

"You're severely dehydrated," she tells Elaine. "You've been sweating all day. You're soaked. You need food and liquid."

But Elaine, in her delirium, cannot even swallow a sip of water. It dribbles out the side of her mouth as soon as Morgan pours it in, sends her friend into a coughing fit. After a quick trip to the supply closet, she pulls out a spare nutrient bag and IV, as if Elaine is suddenly a Block, and puts the needle into Elaine's arm.

"You'll thank me for this later," she tells her friend.

The cold prick of the needle on Elaine's arm seems to bring her out of her stupor for a moment.

"Morgan?" she says, as if not sure where she is, or if she is awake or dreaming.

"I'm right here. You'll be fine. Just rest."

Elaine says something, but it sounds like nonsense.

"I'm sorry, I couldn't hear you."

"I've been having weird dreams."

"You're in Miami, in the group home. But you've come down with something."

"I've been having a lot of dreams," Elaine says again.

"You'll be fine. Just rest."

"I'm scared."

"There's no reason to be scared. You'll be okay."

But as she says it, Morgan wonders if her friend is frightened of having more of the dreams she says she has been having, or of dying. There is no good way to ask such questions without reminding someone of their mortality, and so she says nothing.

"I don't want to die," Elaine says.

"You won't. You'll be fine. You'll feel better in the morning."

"I don't want to die."

"Stop talking like that."

But then Elaine mutters a string of words that might be full sentences, but Morgan can only make out bits and pieces: "In my dreams... at the end... they come for me in my sleep... with me... at the end... never wake up."

"Shhh," Morgan soothes, pulling the blankets up to her friend's chin. "You'll be better in the morning, I promise. Now, rest."

It isn't until she eats and brushes her teeth that she realizes it's past midnight. The moon is already beyond the windows, where the tops of the walls meet the gym's ceiling. The morning rounds usually begin in less than six hours. She sets her alarm to go off an hour later than normal, then closes her eyes.

As tired as she is, it's difficult to quiet her mind.

What will I do if Elaine dies and I'm left to take care of everyone by myself? How can I take care of all of these people day after day?

Her parents would scold her if they were there and knew her concerns were more about being alone than of her friend's well-being. As sleep comes over her, she makes a mental note to e-mail Daniel, her friend in Los Angeles, and ask him how he dealt with it when he became the last caretaker there.

And then sleeps comes.

4

Elaine is bedridden all of the next day. As Morgan finishes her rounds for the night, it begins raining again. Exhausted, Morgan falls onto her mattress and listens to the water hitting the metal roof. It's the only sound she knows of that is peaceful and relaxing, yet is able to make her heart quicken and her breath stop.

She likes the sound because it reminds her of her childhood, when she would sit on her bed with a book and watch the rain bounce off the windows. Without even asking if Morgan wanted some, her mother would appear in the doorway with hot chocolate. The entire time she sipped from the warm cup, she would hear the sound of water running off the roof into the gutters. The thought still makes her feel warm inside.

But the sound also makes her entire body stiffen. This is because she knows it's a matter of time until a hurricane lands directly on the city and destroys the group home. Every year, a string of hurricanes seem to miss Miami just to the east or west, never directly overhead unless it has weakened enough to be considered a tropical storm.

If a genuine hurricane does land on top of them, the metal roof will be ripped off and thrown a mile down the road. They would all be dead in a matter of days. Without a roof, without a real shelter, she and Elaine will have to abandon the remaining Blocks to the elements and seek cover for themselves. This is something she knows she isn't capable of doing. Instead, she would remain in what is left of the building, because that is where her wards are. (She isn't sure, but she thinks Elaine would choose to stay there, too, even though it would mean their certain death.)

There is a basic truth to nature that makes this choice necessary: if she lives with the Blocks when everything is okay, she shouldn't abandon them when everything goes to hell. This is the reason marriage vows speak of the good times and the bad, through sickness and in health. If you are truly devoted to something, you don't give up just so you can preserve yourself.

This idea will keep her with her Blocks even as she and Elaine come down with colds, impossible to avoid without a roof, colds that, at their age, could very well be lethal. The Blocks will be sick too, of course. She will stay with them through all of this.

For the rest, those who survive the initial wave of germs, there are the vultures. Vultures can smell death. It will only be a day or two until the first birds appear on the ledge where the roof used to be. As soon as they take count of the dead, of the sheer volume of raw meat available for pecking, they will descend. Seeing that their dinner puts up no fight, even more scavengers will appear. The animals will eat until they are fat, not caring if their meal is dead due to the storm or to sickness, or even if it is dead at all—the Block's beating heart means nothing to a vulture.

It would be pointless for Morgan to try and scare these creatures away. She could hobble toward them and make them scatter, but they would only fly to another corner of the shelter so many times before they realized she wasn't a threat. It takes Morgan two minutes to walk from one quadrant to another. That's two minutes for the vultures to find a new target and tear away chunks of flesh from helpless Blocks. And even if she made her way toward them as fast as she was able, a different group of vultures would quickly return to the spot she just left.

"Shooo!" she would scream, sobbing as her friends had strips of skin gobbled up.

The fight would be futile. And, to add insult to injury, it is a fight she would only be able to carry on for four or five minutes before she was too tired and light-headed and needed to sit down. She would be forced to rest on a bed in the same building with the Blocks who were being eaten alive by the scourge of the earth. If she rested for too long, if she grew weak from defending everyone else, the vultures might get her as well.

All of this because a storm took their roof off.

Looking back, she wonders why the blizzards of Boston and Chicago seemed scarier than the hurricanes in Miami and New Orleans. Why did people flee from one natural disaster just to flock towards another? Instead of racing south, having all of the final settlements as close to the equator as possible, there could have been a coordinated effort to have final settlements in Seattle, Chicago, or New York. Why did everyone ignore the mudslides and fires and earthquakes in California and the numerous hurricanes in Florida? Just because it was warmer? That didn't make any sense.

Fewer people would have been stuck on the roads if they had just stayed in the northern settlements. Fewer people would have died along the way. But she knows it goes against human nature to want to stay in places like Seattle or Boston when you see more empty houses each day. The population will eventually dwindle away everywhere—people understand this, but they move in packs anyway. Even though the same decline in population eventually occurred in Los Angeles and Miami too, the journey south made everyone feel like they were somehow outracing time.

Time, in terms of waking up each day, is nothing more than death itself. People migrating south would still one day watch everyone they knew grow old and pass away, before they too died, but knowing you had gone in the same direction as everyone else must have offered a sense of comfort.

She knows this because she was one of the masses that never questioned moving south. Her parents decided it was time to move and they moved. That was it.

But now she's in a geographic region that, for a couple of months each year, has a series of storms that threaten her destruction. And they only miss because of luck. It's a matter of time until luck runs out and there is a direct hit. With nature, everything is a matter of time. She imagines a series of storms all lined up, all targeted at Miami. But one after another, they all veer away at the last minute, one to the east, one to the west, each one tearing away huge segments of the country in its path, flooding lands forgotten by man, all the while only giving her a barrage of rain until the winds slow and, eventually, go back to normal.

Although there is no longer a weatherman showing storm charts on the evening news, Morgan can still view the satellite images and computer-generated storm predictions online. The satellites still track each storm and pass the information to the National Weather Service's website. The charts show the eye of the storm as a circle and then various colored lines depicting possible projected paths, calculated by the computers, as the storm makes its way towards land.

Each storm that misses the group home raises the chance that one will eventually not veer off, will land squarely on them. And when it does, the Block home will be torn apart. She is sure of this. And once it's gone, the Miami settlement will vanish like all the rest.

She thinks it miraculous that throughout all of this, throughout her current situation, she is still able to remember the thunderstorms of her childhood and the smell of her mother's hot chocolate. Is that a sign from above that she is protected by a guardian angel? Or is it part of her nature, as a survivor, that even during the worst of times she can remember better moments and be comforted by them? Is it a sign that all worries are forgotten when you get to heaven, or is it nothing more than a natural instinct to reminisce when you know the end is approaching?

Getting out of bed, she goes and checks on Elaine.

"These storms are going to be the end of us," her friend says in a rare moment of lucidity.

"You just worry about getting healthy," Morgan says. "I'll worry about the storms."

Elaine begins crying then, and it's not until she speaks that Morgan has any idea what is upsetting her: "I'm sorry you have to go through all of this by yourself. When I'm gone, please remember me as the person that was laughing with you as we made up stories about all these people. Don't remember me like this. And please don't be mad at me for leaving you here by yourself."

Morgan doesn't know what to say to this, so, as is her custom, she regrettably says nothing at all, only holds her friend's hand and listens to the rain as it continues to fall. The storm helps blot out the sound of Elaine's crying.

"Why did you start creating names and lives for all of the Blocks?" Morgan says, finally having something she thinks is worth saying to Elaine, but when she looks down, her friend is breathing softly, her eyes twitching ever so slightly. Asleep.

She begins to stand, then thinks better of it and remains at Elaine's side. As she watches, Elaine's eyelids flutter ever so slightly. The corners of her mouth twitch.

"It's okay," Morgan says, stroking her friend's forehead. "I'm here. There's nothing to be afraid of."

But her friend keeps flinching in her sleep, and after a minute Morgan stands to continue making her rounds.

5

Elaine will be better today; she has to be.

That's Morgan's first thought when she wakes up.

Her second is not as hopeful: *Why did we spend all this time creating stories for everyone around us instead of discussing what would happen when one of us died and left the other alone?*

After all, their game only started when George, the last male caretaker, walked out of the gymnasium, never to return, and left the two of them to care for everyone by themselves. Had Elaine known what would eventually happen? Had she seen the writing on the wall, that it was a matter of time until either she died and left Morgan alone, or else Morgan died and it was Elaine who was left to care for everyone? Is that why she spent so much time crafting stories for the people all around her, because it took her thoughts away from what would happen next?

The closest she ever saw anyone get to mentioning the topic was when George, back when there were still four caretakers left, had stood in front of the many rows of Blocks in the gymnasium and whispered to himself, "I don't want to be the final one."

With the air conditioning off, his statement travelled across the room to where Morgan was able to hear it. The idea, spoke aloud, was so terrifying she had actually shivered.

Without realizing Morgan had heard him, George had closed his eyes, maybe envisioning a way to keep from being the last caretaker in the facility, and then grunted and opened his eyes and started moving around again.

For a minute, all Morgan could do was stand there with her mouth open. Only when Elaine tapped her on the shoulder and asked what she was thinking about did Morgan erase the comment from her memory and continue on with her day. There was no way she would be the one to bring up the subject after that. Not even with Elaine.

As she approaches Elaine's bed, Morgan says, "See? I told you that you'd feel better in the morning."

She speaks in her most cheerful voice because Elaine needs a positive attitude more than ever. Every part of Morgan's body is sore. Her knees ache. So does her back. Her hands often seize up. Going to bed later than normal, taking care of all of the Blocks by herself, has been tougher than she imagined. But it's important to let Elaine know everything will be okay.

When she sees her friend, though, she gasps. The tube allowing the nutrient bag to provide Elaine with water and nutrition has fallen out—or was pulled out. A small puddle of liquid is on the ground where the nutrient bag drips away its hydration.

Elaine's lips are grey. Her fingers are light blue. Her eyes are open, staring at the ceiling as though that was the last thing she was interested in, but they are glassy and still, focusing on nothing.

"Elaine?"

She does not expect a response, but that does not keep her from repeating her friend's name.

"Elaine? Come on, Elaine."

She puts an ear to Elaine's mouth to listen for breathing. Nothing. She takes Elaine's wrist in her hands and feels for a pulse. Nothing.

"Elaine?"

Now she's only talking to hear her own voice because

it's the only thing that can comfort her, keep her from breaking down.

"Elaine?"

She takes Elaine's hand in her own. However, while her fingers wrap around her friend's palm and squeeze, Elaine's fingers remain only slightly curled, do not offer any warmth, do not encircle Morgan's hand to let her know everything will be okay. They are lifeless.

"Elaine?"

A normal person can survive between three and five days without water. In Elaine's condition—ninety-three old, already sick and dehydrated—it would only take a couple of hours. It's very possible the tube came out right after Morgan went to sleep. It's also possible, even if the nutrient bag had stayed connected, that Elaine would have died anyway.

Morgan rubs her friend's arm where the IV had been. A slight bruise remains on Elaine's forearm, pinpointing the spot where her life might have been saved. There is no intelligent reason for this gesture, nothing that can make a difference, but it makes her feel like maybe she can rub life right back into her friend's body. She might as well be rubbing her friend's feet or washing her hair, but she is desperate.

"I should have sat up with you. I should have made sure you didn't pull the tube out. I should have done something else." She says this to the entire gymnasium, as if defending her need for sleep to the jury of Blocks she is surrounded by.

The only response she gets is the click of the air conditioning unit as it kicks on to provide relief from the warm Miami mornings.

"Oh my God," she says, looking around.

Sixty-four bodies surround her. Distracted, her fingers relax. Elaine's hand immediately falls to the side of the cot, where it hangs without swaying.

"My God," she says again.

She is alone. For the first time in her life, she is utterly and truly alone. With her are a gymnasium full of people relying on her to stay alive. Four quadrants of sixteen bodies depending on her. Sixty-four souls with her as their protector. And yet she is alone.

"Oh my God," she says again.

Behind her, she hears the imaginary voices of over fifty people say, in unison, "You aren't alone. You have us."

"Is that why the game was so important?" she says, looking down at Elaine.

What else can she say? Her head falls into her hands. She sobs over the body of the only other person who knew what she was going through, who helped care for the Blocks. It is only when she has cried so long, no new tears able to fall, that she remembers to brush her hand over her friend's eyelids.

The eyes, which had been staring up at the rafters, or beyond, finally close.

6

The forklift starts on the first try. Even so, Morgan sits atop it, motionless, until she assesses what she is supposed to do and judges whether or not she can do it. A wood block has been added to the pedal so her miniature legs can reach it. It takes both of her hands to move a lever that a normal driver is supposed to be able to throw around with ease. She only knows how to operate the damn thing because she watched George use it so many times.

"Dear lord," she mutters.

The machine's loud rumble cancels any noise created by the power generator and air conditioner. A pile of blankets conceal her friend's body so she doesn't have to see it. The same stack of blankets makes it impossible for Morgan not to think about the times, as a kid, when she hid in the laundry during games of hide-and-go-seek, waiting to see if her mother could find her. Now, the bundle of blankets hides a body from sight before it goes into the incinerator.

There is no other way to dispose of bodies. Certainly, she cannot dig a grave. The body has to be removed from the area way, though, or else disease will creep in and spread throughout the entire gymnasium. And she can't simply abandon the body outside the gymnasium. Predators would be attracted to the remains and begin circling the building she calls home. Instead, anyone who dies is carried to the flames.

The duty used to belong to George. Any time a Block passed away, George would climb up into the forklift, position it in place, and take the body to the fire. Every once in a while he had to reposition the forklift three or four times before it was aligned with the bed correctly, and Morgan and Elaine realized George's eyesight must have been failing him more than he was willing to admit.

"Would you like help?" they would ask him.

"I'm fine," he always replied, moving his thick glasses up on his nose and squinting.

"Are you sure?"

But instead of answering, he would shake his head and narrow his eyes and try again. Some people, no matter how old they get, don't want to admit their limitations.

The very last time George took a body to the incinerator, he powered up the forklift and moved it into place. But when he raised the forklift's arms, only the back end of the bed raised, and before George saw his mistake and could pull the lever back, the bed had been flipped upside down. The poor body that had been atop the bed had gone crashing over the side, head first, and was left in an ugly position that not even the most dedicated yoga practitioner should attempt. If the Block hadn't already been dead, it would have been then.

"Damn it!" George had yelled.

"Let me help you," Morgan had said, but George was already shifting the forklift's gears again. Instead of getting out and saving the body some dignity and respect, George had lowered the forklift's arms so they were at ground level, and then he cranked another lever so the machine moved forward, pushing the body and the bed across the floor instead of carrying it. By the time it was halfway across to the door and the incinerator outside, a pile of dust had collected under the poor Block.

"It's okay," Elaine had told him after the whole thing was over. "We all get old. One of us can start doing the forklift."

The next day, though, George had opened the gymnasium door, walked away, and was never seen again. Some people are inclined to face the harsh realities of life, while others simply are not. Or, as Elaine had put it, "That old bastard should have just admitted he was blind as a bat and stopped punishing himself."

Morgan is older than she ever imagined herself being, but her eyesight has not deteriorated. Her sense of smell is almost gone. With it, her sense of taste. Parts of her are deadened to sensation while other parts constantly cry for a reprieve from her chores. But she can see exactly where she needs the forklift to be in order to carry her friend away. She doesn't even need to squint.

The forklift's arms move under the blankets and scoop up the hidden body beneath them.

How absurd I must look, she thinks. *An old woman in the driver seat of a warehouse machine.*

She imagines one of her Blocks calling out, "If you think this is bad, I once had to drive a replica of the Batmobile all the way from Boston to Baltimore."

"Not now," she says, determined to get this job over with as quickly as possible.

Thankfully, the forklift's motor drowns out the noise of Elaine's body catching on fire and then sizzling into ash. When the forklift's arms come out of the flames, they are slightly orange, like a welder's anvil.

She tries not to think about being the only person left to care for an entire gymnasium full of bodies. But she knows that isn't the only thing bothering her; she is also the final normal person in the entire city. There's a chance George is out there in the city, alone. Not a strong chance, though. As bad as his eyesight was, he wouldn't be able to see the buttons on a food processor and would starve. And that's if he was able to see the potholes on his way to another home. Probably, he would only get a few hundred feet before stepping right into a hole and either twisting his ankle or falling face first onto the concrete. It's likely he died a day or two after abandoning the shelter. There is no telling what animals stalk the city streets looking for food.

Daniel, in Los Angeles, is the only other person she knows of in the entire world who is still alive. This, more than anything, is what she tries not to think about because it means all the other final settlements have gone quiet. And if they have gone quiet, it's a matter of time until hers does as well.

The seemingly endless amount of cots in front of her offers all the distraction she needs. If she doesn't make her way through all four quadrants each day, someone else will begin to suffer. This thought is what pushes her up and down the aisles without a chance to stand in front of Elaine's empty bed and feel sorry for herself. As she makes her way through the rows, her fingertips touch the heads and feet of the bodies she cares for. Such smooth skin. So soft. There is no scientific proof, but she has always thought that everyone, Block or not, is healthier if they have human contact. Even the simple touch of a human hand once a day.

Maybe, she thinks, life is about the first time you touch another person, and the last. This thought is comforting.

For one day, at least, it's easy not to focus on her aching back as she bends over each Block. It's easy to ignore her rumbling stomach. She knows she must be tired, must be hungry, but doesn't feel it. She moves from bed to bed in anticipation of e-mailing Daniel as soon as she is done. She will not allow herself to stop halfway through the rows of Blocks. It would be like opening Christmas presents early. She needs something to look forward to in order to get through the day.

Finally, when she is finished, she washes her hands and puts food into her belly. If asked the next day, she wouldn't even be able to say what meal she ate. She has learned that there are few things you really need to focus on and many things you can get through without much thought.

Finally, eagerly, she moves to her computer and opens her e-mail. She looks for the last time she sent him a message and frowns when she sees it has been more than a month. His latest e-mail to her, from two days before that, is still there, still waiting for a real response.

The only thing she had written at the time was: *Soooo busy. Really sorry to hear you're alone. Wish I had time to write more. Will write again when things slow down.*

Part of her blames the lack of a response on how busy she has been. But she knows he was the final remaining caretaker at the Los Angeles group home for the last month, meaning he has been even busier than her. Yet he still found time to e-mail someone. The other part of her blames her lack of response on not knowing what to say to him. That sounds immature and childlike, she knows that. It's not a quality she is proud to display as an old woman. She is no better than a teenage girl who has received a love note and doesn't know how to tell a boy who is interested in her that she doesn't share the same feelings, and so simply tried to brush him off.

Daniel's message had been straight forward enough. In only a few lines he had stated that the only other caretaker in the Los Angeles facility had passed away the night before, and that now he was left alone to care for roughly forty Blocks by himself. He ended the e-mail by asking how she was doing, how the Miami home was doing as a whole, and by stating that, as far as he knew, his Los Angeles group home and her Miami group home were the only two remaining in the country.

Instead of writing anything meaningful, she had been a coward and said she was overwhelmed with her own Blocks.

There were a lot of things she had thought to say in her response. She could have told him that not only were they the last two settlements in the States, but also that her contact in the Lisbon group home had gone quiet six months earlier and that Europe may not have anyone left either. She could have told him that her pen pal in Caracas had gone silent nine weeks ago. There was a very good chance no one was alive in South America either. As far as she knew, she and Daniel were the last two living people in the entire world.

Except for all of their Blocks.

Every time she has the thought about being the last person in Miami or on the East Coast, she corrects herself and includes the bodies she cares for, complete with their made-up lives and personalities.

She wonders what Daniel will think to finally get a real response from her. She will not tell him right away that she is only replying in depth now that she is in the same situation he has been in for over a month. Maybe she can offer him some sense of comfort, and maybe he can tell her it's not too bad being the last person in an entire city.

She is usually careful in crafting her e-mails, strict about being grammatically correct, using the active voice instead of the passive, sounding like she has everything under control. Tonight, though, she is too restless to have someone to communicate with, too eager to send her e-mail so she can receive another message from him. And so she doesn't even check for misspelled words or run-on sentences, she just types it up and clicks SEND as quickly as her gnarled fingers will let her.

She does not ask him how he thinks life is measured. Nor does she ask if he ever thinks about what happens after you die. Those things can wait for another day. Tonight, she merely wants to know how he is getting on by himself and what it's like to know there is nobody else—she corrects herself: no other regular people—around for hundreds or maybe thousands of miles.

7

Following her high school graduation, Morgan went on a road trip across the country. Now, as her days come to a close, she thinks about that trip more than any other part of her life.

For two months, Morgan and her best friend drove from city to city, state to state, to see all the things America is known for. Her best friend, Anna, was two years older than she was. Being that she was the youngest normal person in her town, all of Morgan's friends were older than her. All the girls her own age were Blocks.

The roads were still good enough back then to travel across the country. Such freedom. This was before the migrations really caught on and a flow of people moved continuously south across the lands until there was no place further they could go. Only Maine and parts of Canada had begun trickling downward as Morgan and Anna made their way through the states. They saw lines of vehicles, hundreds of cars long, filing from one city to another.

"Wouldn't you rather go to the beach for senior week?" her mother had asked before the trip ever started.

"No, I'd rather get to see everything before it's too late."

It helped make the decision easy for her when her

friends all heard from their older brothers and sisters that beach week had lost its appeal many years earlier. There was no point going to Ocean City just to cry over how the world was changing. She imagined herself as the only person on the boardwalk, the only kid on a roller coaster, and didn't want that thought to become a reality.

Planning for the trip had almost been as much fun as the trip itself. For a few weeks, at least, the entire world seemed open to her, like she could do anything she wanted and there were no limits. The maps laid out in front of her, full of highways and cities, reassured her that this was true.

"I want to make sure we see Seattle and Los Angeles and all of Texas," Anna said.

"I want to see Mount Rushmore, the St. Louis Arch, and the Statue of Liberty," Morgan added.

For an entire week, they did nothing but point to various places on a map and add destinations to their wish list. Their proposed agenda, by any standard, was impressive. Except for Kentucky, Iowa, Utah, and Maine, they planned to travel through every state in the continental United States. Even at eighteen years of age, Morgan knew she would never get to see Hawaii or Alaska. That portion of the world, like Europe, was already closed off to her.

Her parents had allowed the sightseeing trip through the country, but they wouldn't let her entertain the thought of an adventure on another continent. Even though both of her parents had backpacked through Europe during their younger years, there were too many rumors of tourists getting stranded over there when an airline or cruise ship closed their doors and people didn't have a way to get back home.

"But, Mom."

"No. Do you know how often they have labor strikes over there? And that was before the Great De-evolution. Now that they know they're the only ones who can do the job, they can make any demands they want. What would you do if you got there and then all the pilots went on strike, or worse, they never showed up to work again? How would you get back here?"

Even as an impetuous teenager, she knew her mother was right. And, in fact, during the leg of her trip through the Southwest, she saw reports that there were massive labor strikes across France, Spain, and Italy as workers tried to squeeze whatever income they could out of their employers before their occupations became outdated. For months, there was no trash collection, no subway service, and no taxi drivers in much of Europe. At one of the many cyber-cafés along their trip, where Morgan and Anna checked their e-mail, Morgan's mother included a link to a story covering the unrest in Europe, her way of saying "I told you so" without using those specific words.

Friends, especially young friends, are meant to bicker and get on each other's nerves. But for two months, Morgan and Anna got along fabulously. When they both had an opinion about the next place they should stop, it was always the same place. When either of them didn't have a preference one way or the other, they happily deferred to their friend. They agreed on everything, from their route, to which city they slept in each night, to where they ate breakfast.

They saw the Grand Canyon, the Alamo, and Niagara Falls. They saw Hoover Dam, Rocky Mountain National Park, and Cape Canaveral. For Morgan, though, nothing could match the Grand Canyon. As far as she could see, the earth was torn apart with rocks and caves. It was the power of nature. Something as simple as water had carved out a great portion of the land, leaving miles and miles of beautiful rock formations, crevices, and gorges. If water could do that to the land, what chance did she have of leaving her own mark on the world? She was only a girl—a young woman; she could never compete with simple forces like air and water and gravity.

The most she could do was use a stone to scratch her initials into one of the rock formations. The rain would wash away her work within a week. It was a trivial reminder of how incidental her life was compared to the water, which had formed the canyons in the first place, and would continue to be on Earth millions of years after Morgan was gone. In front of her was proof that the entire world could be changed by the simplest of powers. But instead of making her life feel unimportant, the great rock formations, red under the sun, gave her a sense of awe. She felt lucky just to have a chance to live in this world where such sights could be seen. It took her breath away.

Looking out at the stretch of orange and red canyon, Anna said something, but Morgan didn't hear what the words had been.

"What?"

"I said it's amazing, isn't it?"

"Yes."

After offering the acknowledgment, Morgan went back to staring at the expanse of colored stone all around her. It was a place she could spend the rest of her life. She would be perfectly happy to set up a tent and wake up each day in front of those rocks.

"Ready to go?" Anna asked.

Without saying anything, Morgan stood up and brushed the dirt off her shorts.

For the rest of the road trip, though, she found herself thinking of those rocks and that canyon. No matter what other monuments or landmarks they saw, she would envision the expanse of earth carved out by nothing more than water. Anna said her favorite part of the trip had been the great redwoods and sequoias in California, trees so gigantic that other trees resembled nothing more than grass under their giant uncles. But Morgan knew, even as Anna mentioned the colossuses, that they didn't hold the same power over her friend that the Grand Canyon held over her. She was thinking of it when they passed through Dallas and Houston, and she was still thinking about it when they passed through New Orleans.

And she thinks about it now anytime she feels overwhelmed, which is quite often. Surrounded by Blocks, each of them withered and grey, like herself, she takes a deep breath and remembers how great the expanse of carved earth had been, that simple droplets of water, combined together into streams and rivers and lakes, could cut the earth away into something more beautiful than anything man could ever make with his two hands and his great intellect. These visions of the canyon allow her to remember that whatever is upsetting her, whatever seems like it's too much for one person to handle, pales in comparison to the forces all around her. Her ordeal is nothing compared to what has happened across the earth for millions of years. After all, these final moments are only a grain of dust in the timespan it took for those canyons to be formed.

Most often, the Grand Canyon comes back to her as she makes her way through the many rows of Blocks. Whenever she feels too old to reposition a body, or when her knees start to ache, she thinks of those bloodshot rocks, those burgundy canyons, and her hands stop their shaking. She even remembered it as the forklift carried Elaine's body to the incinerator. As Elaine's hair dangled off the forklift's arm, Morgan thought back to how the sunset had competed with the earth for which could be a brighter color of red until everything in front of her looked like Mars, a place too amazingly beautiful to be real.

She thought of the Grand Canyon yesterday as it rained straight through from morning until night, and, looking out at all the rows of people depending on her, she thinks of it again now.

"If you liked the Grand Canyon," Aristotle, her world traveler Block, says, "you would love Mount Kilimanjaro."

"I wish I could have gotten a chance to see it," she says. Usually, she hates it when people tell her what she would like and what she wouldn't like, but when Aristotle says these things, she knows he is probably right and takes his word for it.

Aristotle is one of her favorite Blocks. Unlike her, he was lucky enough to backpack through every continent (except for Antarctica) and got to see all the places Morgan only read about. He saw Big Ben in London, the Eiffel Tower in Paris, the Pantheon in Rome. But more than those tourist attractions, he attended soccer matches in England and Brazil, got swallowed up in the crowd's enthusiasm. He ate chocolate frog legs in a back-alley Parisian café and spider legs in Australia. And, in the middle of the night, he was able to sneak under the gates to the Coliseum and walk in the areas cordoned off to visitors. Every part of the world unlocked itself for him. He is the envy of every other Block in the shelter because of all the things he has managed to see.

"There are some truly amazing places in this world," he tells her.

"Yes, there are."

As she moves to the next bed—her rounds don't stop just because she wants to reminisce—she thinks of what the Grand Canyon must have looked like millions of years earlier when it was part of a sea.

Maybe life can be measured by the first thing that takes your breath away, and by the last time you remember what that feeling was like.

8

She doesn't let herself check for a response from Los Angeles until the next day's chores are done. This means taking care of all of the Blocks. Rather than getting accustomed to the task at hand, it quickly wears her down.

At least there isn't one for every year I've been alive, she thinks.

"How are Blocks different from Congress?" Cindy says. Without waiting for a response, Morgan's comedian adds, "One can't do anything for themselves and has nothing to contribute to society, and the other has you to take care of them!"

"Come on, Cindy."

"Hey, a lot of comedians get funnier with age," Cindy says, her lips not moving as the imaginary words are formed.

This thought does not cheer Morgan up.

"Of course," Cindy says, with regrettable grimness, "a lot of people don't get funnier the older they get. They just die."

"Thanks," Morgan says before walking to the next bed.

But Cindy isn't done: "Knock, knock."

Morgan groans, but plays along. "Who's there?"

"Block."

"Block who?"

"Block who just made you sit here and listen to a bad joke!"

Morgan walks away without replying.

Everything she does is set against a numerical standard by which she can measure her progress. *Only one more Block until this row is one hundred percent done.* Two hours later: *Only one more Block until this quadrant is done.* Four hours later: *Only one more row to go until three quadrants have been cared for.*

Everything is about the percent she has completed, not the percent she still has to go. It is easier to face the challenge ahead if she is almost done with each portion she keeps track of; if she were to get to the end of the first row and, instead of considering an entire section as almost being complete, look ahead to the other fifteen rows she still has to get through, she would quickly feel overwhelmed. Better to focus on tiny gains and progress until the entire thing is done.

It is eleven at night before she finishes. She doesn't bother with her own dinner before rushing to the computer. The final Block's lips are still moist from the wet cloth she has rubbed across his face as her computer wakes up and her e-mail is opened.

But as soon as it appears, her chest is deflated. There is no reply from Daniel.

She chides herself for counting on an immediate response after she herself did not reply to his previous e-mail for over a month. She types a quick follow up.

> *Please write to me as soon as you have a chance. I know you must be busy. I know how overwhelming it must be. But please write to me and tell me everything is okay. I need to hear from you.*

She does not like to beg. The last time she did something like this was when she was sixteen and was madly in love with a boy who acted like he was too cool to talk to her. The feeling of assumed rejection, the feeling of desperation, need only be experienced once for someone to never want to feel it a second time.

I'm an old woman, she thinks, *what do I care of coming off as scared and hopeless?*

She remembers how her own grandparents could get away with anything, for no better reason than they were old. Their response had always been, "If being headstrong in our old age is our worst quality, then sue us." She tries to use the same argument for herself, but knows she is not headstrong, only panicked.

The next day is the same: she forces herself to complete her rounds before checking for a response from Los Angeles. Her body resists the task ahead. Her legs are swollen. Her knuckles are hard balls of cartilage. But she moves forward anyway, hoping her body will feel better once she begins moving around and the muscles warm up. It takes more than three hours—she is already caring for the Blocks in quadrant 2—before her back and legs don't hurt so bad.

The faster she gets through with the Blocks, the faster she can be comforted by Daniel's message. This is why she ignores the groans in her stomach and skips lunch.

With the final Block cleaned, repositioned, and possessing a newly refilled nutrient bag, Morgan shuffles across the floor as quickly as she can to her computer. It seems to take forever for the screen to load. She fidgets with her fingernails while the screen goes from black to blue and then to the picture she has as her wallpaper—Earth from outer space a hundred years earlier. The entire globe is illuminated by tiny dots of lights—cities—coming together to make the planet look as though it's glowing. The image reminds her of how much life was once in every corner of the world.

Without realizing it, she has picked away pieces of a fingernail until it's dripping blood on her clothes and on the keyboard. She lets it continue to bleed without a second thought.

Finally, her e-mail is up. Her finger clicks as fast as it

can so her inbox will appear.

The wind is knocked out of her. Once again, there is no response.

Maybe he's ignoring me on purpose to get back at me for not replying to his last e-mail quickly enough.

But she knows this isn't the case. People don't act like that once they become adults. They certainly don't act that way as senior citizens. And, alone himself, he would know all too well what she is going through. He would have to be heartless not to reply and provide some reassurance and comfort. The thought reminds her of how painfully immature she was in not giving him a better response earlier. She was the very thing she doesn't want him to be.

He must be too busy.

She repeats the thought in her mind because the alternative is that he isn't busy at all; he is gone. Just like all the others. This idea, when it sneaks into her head, makes her chest heavy, makes it difficult for her to breathe. She has never had a panic attack, does not know what they are like, but if anything can cause her to have one, it would be the realization that she is not only alone in Miami, alone on the East Coast, but alone in the world. There is not a single other normal person alive on the planet.

Did she contribute to his end? If she had done something as simple as email him back and allow herself to be vulnerable and admit her own fears, would he have had someone to share his own burden with? Was that all he needed?

A shudder goes through her entire body. She retches, but no vomit comes up. A shiver racks her. Her hands are shaking.

The last regular living person in the world, she thinks. And then: *Please, God, no.*

It begins raining. Within seconds, the rain goes from being nonexistent to pouring down. It is quickly matched by a howling wind.

From across the gymnasium, Cindy calls out, "Just

41

when you didn't think things could get any worse!"

The metal roof whines under the force of the wind. If just a little bit of wind can work its way under the metal sheets, the roof will be gone.

Not even Cindy thinks this possibility is funny. The comedian remains silent the rest of the night as the storm roars overhead.

9

Amazingly, there is no damage from the storm. Not that she can tell, at least. Of course, she doesn't venture out of the main room of the Block shelter anymore, except to use the restroom and to take trash out to the incinerator. It's possible that the main part of the school, where the classrooms once were, suffered severe damage from the wind and now resembles a Greek ruin. All she cares about is that the gymnasium, where kids once played dodge ball and attended pep rallies, is still intact.

When she thinks of the history of the room she works in each day, she can't help but think back to how long it's been since she was one of the kids sitting in the bleachers. Somehow, the stench of floor polish and sweaty kids, of popcorn and hot dogs, seems to remain in certain corners of the vast room. She knows this is a trick of her mind, though. In her old age, she can't even smell the urine, shit, and body odor that must cover every part of the group home. There is no way she can actually pick up the odor of something from decades earlier.

In a similar gymnasium, a lifetime ago, she was one of many uninterested teenagers who was forced to listen to an old man speak about the importance of doing well in school, going to a good college, and getting a decent job. Didn't he know that the Great De-evolution meant none of those things mattered anymore?

Instead of taking notes and paying careful attention to what was said, all of the kids had day dreamed of what the Great De-evolution might mean for them. No need to find a job! A life free of responsibility. How naïve they had all been to think the end of man would make life more simple for them.

After the Blocks appeared and the last generation of normal kids finished school, this gymnasium, like other school gyms around the country, was gutted of its bleachers and turned into a factory for making food processors. The same adults who taught geography, grammar, and mathematics, took off their slacks and button-up shirts and came to work wearing sweatpants and t-shirts. They were joined by day-care workers and part-time babysitters—people who needed something to do with their time. Anyone who wanted to stay busy but no longer had a profession needed by the aging population appeared at the factory doors. Eventually, mailmen, landscapers, and taxi drivers showed up as well.

A day came when food processors had been shipped out all over the country and the factory was no longer needed, just as the gymnasium had once become obsolete. At the same time, waves of new families were traveling south each day. Fifty years earlier, at the peak of the migrations, a thousand new Blocks arrived in Miami every month. Some were abandoned in city streets by people who could no longer take care of them. Some were rescued from those who preyed on the weak and defenseless. These bodies had to be put somewhere. So the assembly lines were torn apart and the giant room was gutted once more, but only so it could be packed with cots.

That was also when the gymnasium was outfitted with a new air conditioning system. The previous system would break and need repairs every two or three years. As the population grew older, however, and as the room became filled with weak and feeble bodies, even a day without air conditioning in the hot Miami summers could mean hundreds of deaths. The same bill that produced reliable power generators and incinerators for each house in the country made sure new AC units were installed in each group home. Without it, Morgan and everyone around her would already be dead.

But there is much more to the school than simply the gymnasium. There are classrooms, administrative offices, locker rooms. She does not wander the halls, though, does not leave the giant room where her Blocks are. There is nothing to be gained from looking into old classrooms where kids used to raise their hands to answer questions or look down at their desk if they didn't want to be called on. Some classrooms probably still have framed portraits of each President. Each photograph, though, has faded beyond recognition. Other rooms have maps of the world. But the maps are outdated; the countries on them no longer exist in any meaningful way. Still other rooms have band equipment that has rusted and warped over the decades.

There is no point to visiting the administrative portion of the building, where the principal and vice principal would lecture misbehaving students on the importance of not having their bad behavior recorded on a make-believe "permanent record." There is no telling what might lie in the janitor's closet.

For all she knows, every part of the school, save the gymnasium, might have already been turned back over to the wilderness the way the school's parking lot has been. All it takes is one broken window and the weeds, dirt, grass, animals, and everything else that was supposed to be the outside world, quickly becomes part of the inside world.

There are days she wishes a storm would just go ahead and end everything. On the days she is feeling sorry for herself, questioning if she can even provide adequate care to those who depend on her, she wishes it could all be taken out of her control. There is no chance she would end things herself, but if God was ready for her, she wouldn't complain when she was called. A category-5 hurricane would certainly accomplish that.

Other days, she is glad for the time she has, counts herself lucky to have a solid roof over her head and a purpose in her days. These are the times she prays for the storms to leave her alone. She is thankful, even if she is surrounded by people who can't communicate with her, that she has time to think about not only her life, but all life.

It's impossible not to think about your place within the entirety of mankind when you are surrounded by sixty-four mouths that rely wholly and singly on you. She thinks of lions caring for their cubs. She thinks of early cavemen confronting the unknowns of the world as they tried to keep their children alive. And she even thinks of the Earth as a tiny speck in the galaxy, about how, in the end, the sun is not so different from a lioness or a scared man in a cave. Every part of the universe, she thinks, is dependent on something else. It is a beautiful, yet delicate framework. Just look at how quickly dinosaurs vanished from the earth. A single meteor! And look at how it only takes one lifetime for all of mankind to disappear from the planet. Indeed, life is delicate.

When she thinks of her own place in the universe as one microscopic grain of life on one minuscule planet in one tiny solar system, she wonders if there is anything at all to learn from mankind's existence or if the entire thing was nothing more than a cosmic coincidence that has run its course. If she knew for sure that there was a god watching out for her, she would know there were lessons she was supposed to gain from what has taken place during the span of her life. But knowing the great expanse that is out there—billions of stars, trillions of planets—she knows there is nothing truly significant about her place in the cosmos, even if there is a higher power.

Maybe life is measured by the first time you question your place in the world and by the final answer you come up with.

Amongst the rows of Blocks that she and Elaine assigned life stories to, there is a minister, a Zen master, a philosopher, and a therapist. Between the four of them, they should be able to provide some clarity. Instead, each one contradicts the others, leaving her more confused than before.

The minister looks up at the stars and tells her, "Only God could create something so majestic and immense. Who are we to question his work?"

The Zen master looks into the palm of his hand. "It is not only the universe that is infinite, it is each of us. We all have different realities regarding the same events. Your consciousness is timeless and spaceless, too!"

The philosopher looks at one tiny piece of dirt on the floor and says, "That single little crumb is your life. Look at how tiny it is compared to the gymnasium. And think of everything that exists outside these doors."

The therapist frowns and says, "The room is only as big or small as it makes you feel. Oftentimes, a feeling of being overwhelmed during a crisis is due to abandonment issues."

"All four of you, please shut up."

"We're only trying to help," they say in unison.

"Screw off," she says, giving them the finger and walking to a different area of the group home.

This is exactly why she doesn't bother asking them the questions that are always bouncing around in her head; they don't know any more than she does.

10

Denial does not work. Even as she tries to convince herself that he might have stopped checking his e-mail regularly, considering how long it took for her to reply, each passing day makes it a little tougher to hold out hope that Daniel will ever write her again. Time is denial's mortal enemy and is always victorious against it. After a week, she no longer checks her e-mail every night. Another week after that, she forces herself to check but without any expectation of finding a new note. This silence is different from the one she put him through. Hers was vexing, inconsiderate. His, she fears, is permanent.

She didn't reply to his e-mail because she didn't know what to say. How do you tell someone who is all alone that everything will be okay, especially if you aren't sure that it will be? What words can comfort someone who realizes they are completely responsible for so many other lives?

Only now, with Elaine gone, does she too have these fears. Now she understands what Daniel must have been going through when he wanted to hear from her. She still doesn't have the words that could have reassured him, made him believe everything would be okay, but providing any reply at all would have been better than nothing. She knows this now.

Now that it's too late, she thinks, punishing herself.

Getting through each day is a little tougher than it was the day before. Without Elaine, she not only has to take care of the Blocks in her charge, she has to take care of herself, do all of the cleaning, maintenance, everything. When the tasks were split between her and Elaine, they would each care for thirty-two Blocks and then divide the other chores. Morgan would clean their beds and wash the dishes while Elaine prepared meals and emptied any mousetraps. Every once in a while, just for variety, one of them would take care of all four quadrants of Blocks while the other person slept in, relaxed, and rested. This was a rarity, though. Like finding a dollar on the ground. Like seeing a beautiful rainbow. Both of them knew that caring for the entire gymnasium's population wasn't something their bodies could do for an extended period. They were simply too old.

She could use a day of rest now. Each knuckle on every finger aches and, periodically through the day, locks in place until she rubs them loose again. Her legs feel like she has shin splints, the type she used to have after hour-long runs as a teenager, even though all she does now is shuffle from bed to bed. It takes a little longer each day to make it all the way through the rows of Blocks and get to bed. It takes a little more energy. It wears her out.

"Buck up now," Jimbo calls out. "If it was easy, everyone would be doing it."

"That doesn't even make sense," she replies. "No one else is around to do it. And, I might add, I wish it were easy."

All he can offer in return is a stubborn, "Whatever."

It's only after she is sure she will never hear from Daniel that she allows herself to begin replaying her final days with Elaine.

"Don't do that," Jimbo warns. "As soon as you start thinking about the past, old demons will haunt you. Trust me, after I caught the Block Slasher, I—"

"Not now," she says.

"Whatever."

It has been two weeks since her friend passed away. Between looking forward to Daniel's response and taking care of the Blocks from the moment she wakes to the time she goes to bed, she has been able to avoid thinking of the things Elaine said that final night.

"Please... don't let them get me," her friend had whispered. The words echo in Morgan's head as she tries to think of something or someone that may have plagued Elaine's nightmares. Who would she have been afraid of? Who would she need protection from? Maybe her friend was simply an arachnophobe and had dreams of spiders crawling on her skin.

"They come for me... at the end..."

Did Elaine know she was going to die that night? Had she seen something to make her believe she was going to close her eyes and never open them again? Who was coming for her? How did she know it was her end?

At the time, Morgan had discounted the words as the nonsense of someone with an incredibly high fever. Alone now, with nothing to do but replay the final statements, she can only take the words seriously and try to figure out what they might have meant.

Even with these thoughts troubling her, she is so tired she can close her eyes and fall right away to asleep. Her legs buckle. She opens her eyes and catches herself before hitting the ground.

Standing at the sixty-forth bed, she realizes she must have put her head down on the last Block and fallen asleep while still on her feet. She shuffles over to her own bed, gives a groan as she lowers herself onto the skinny mattress, and closes her eyes. The longer she stays up and dwells on whether Elaine's remarks were due to fever-induced hallucinations or were the scared thoughts of a dying woman, the less time she has to rest her body before she must once again start making her way from cot to cot, body to body.

11

She cannot keep up. The first few days of taking care
of all of the Blocks wasn't too bad because the responsibility
was still fresh and she was focused on Elaine's health. The
next week, as she waited for a reply from Daniel, she pushed
through the chores just so she could finish the day by
checking her e-mail. But even then, as she forced her way
through each row of beds in anticipation of the little reward
she allowed herself, she noticed the rounds taking a little
longer each day. The change was almost imperceptible at first.
She finished by eleven o'clock at night. The next day, ten
minutes later. The day after that, eleven-twenty. By the end of
the first week, she wasn't finishing until midnight. After two
weeks, she isn't done cleaning and repositioning the final
Block until one in the morning.

When will it end?

I can't keep doing this, she thinks.

But she persists. Another week goes by. She is tired
before she even starts her rounds. It is two o'clock in the
morning when she finishes. Exhausted, her attention to detail
fades. Late at night, only three Blocks away from being done
for the day, she looks back at the previous Block she has just
finished caring for and realizes she forgot to screw the tube
to the Block's IV back into his nutrient bag. Without it, he

would starve and quickly die.

I must be getting tired. Where is my mind?

Little mistakes keep occurring. In the middle of her rounds, she can't remember which Block she has just finished cleaning and which was to be cared for next. She imagines herself, an old woman shuffling slowly around the room, being recorded on some security monitor in a back office. How absurd she would seem. How futile her task.

I'm killing myself. I can't take this much longer.

She still gets up at six every morning. If she sleeps in after a long day, it just means she either finishes even later the next night, or some of the Blocks go uncared for.

She has barely begun her chores the next day before the first mistake occurs. When she looks back at a Block she has just finished repositioning, she realizes she left the body facedown. The Blocks cannot do anything for themselves; a mouth and nose pressed into a pillow could very well lead to a slow suffocation for the poor man. She shuffles back to the bed, turns the man's face to one side, then moves on to the next cot.

I can't keep doing this. I'm going to drop dead and then everyone here will die.

She spills the contents of an entire nutrient bag on the floor. Clear plasma splashes on two beds, all over her feet, up her legs. Defeated, she walks across the gym and gets a mop. By the time she is done cleaning up the mess she has made in her drowsy, zombie-like stupor, she is an hour behind her already lagging schedule.

I'm not going to get to bed until 4 o'clock. And then the thought: *I can't do this anymore. I just can't.*

The situation does not seem fair. She has only gotten herself into this spot because she lived when everyone else passed away. It is a burden she was never ready for, does not think she could ever be suited for.

She tries to think of a way to continue caring for each Block. Her predicament only exists because she can't move fast enough to tend to so many people. Even though they are sixty-four people that require very little attention, a woman of her age was never meant to perform these chores at all, not to one person, let alone row after row of them. She changes their nutrient bags once a day. This gives them hydration and nutrition. She changes their Block diapers once a day. She washes their bodies every other day. They are repositioned twice a week. This is to prevent bedsores. They used to be moved more frequently, back when there were more care workers. She has given up on brushing their teeth. This was the first sacrifice that had to be made so their collective health was sustained.

But even these simple, basic needs—food, cleanliness—have become too much for one person. Beginning her rounds as soon as she wakes up makes no difference. If she wakes at four in the morning, she starts her rounds. Her conscience does not let her go back to sleep because sleep means all of these people, people who are relying on her, are going without care longer than they should.

There are no vacations. She cannot take days off. There is no one to alternate duties with. She no longer bothers to clean her dirty dishes. She pulls a filthy plate out of the sink and puts new food on it because that saves a couple of minutes.

Naively, she once thought if she merely moved faster, she could still care for each person the way she used to when Elaine was here. There is no pace to quicken, though, when you are ninety-three years old.

Maybe if I only clean them once every three days. Maybe if I only reposition them once a week.

But this is desperation speaking. This line of thought is how the quality of life begins to diminish past the point anyone would consider acceptable. Bedsores will begin to develop if she only cleans them every three days, if she only adjusts their arms and legs a few times each month. Infections will spread. She won't allow that to happen to her Blocks. She has already stopped shaving the men's faces and combing the women's hair. She no longer takes the time to offer a loving caress on each person's hand or cheek. There is nothing else she can cut back on to help get through all the chores for every Block. Yet continuing with such little sleep is not realistic. It will kill her. If she dies, the people she is caring for will all die too.

I can't keep doing this.

Only two thirds of the way through her chores, she is already so exhausted that she needs to put her head on the closest cot and regain her balance. The very real thought crosses her mind that she could crawl into bed next to the Block already positioned there and take a week-long nap. The Block does not move over to make room for her. He does not offer an encouraging smile.

She thinks about lying down on the floor and sleeping there, even though her own bed is only a hundred feet away. Too far when she is this tired. Sleep beckons to her. But she is already struggling to finish her chores in one day; a nap would mean she wouldn't finish until the next morning. And then, the following night, she wouldn't be done until the next afternoon. Any semblance of a 24-hour schedule would be gone. She would find herself working through the night, through the mornings. Without a boundary of time, she would collapse.

I can't keep doing this.

It's not an option to stop at midnight and leave some of the people uncared for. Even if there were only two more Blocks left to be cleaned and fed, she couldn't go to sleep knowing they have to wait for basic care that everyone else has already received. Her conscience wouldn't let her sleep. She could walk back to her own cot, but a voice in the back of her head would keep reminding her of the people who were wearing shit-filled diapers. This thought would force her back out of bed. It's a losing battle. She knows this.

Some days, she thinks the entire group should band together and suffer equally, as long as it means everyone survives. This is how countries unite during wars. It's how families come together after tragedies. But what is the point of sixty-five people (she includes herself, even though she is the caretaker and the only person in the building with a real voice) suffering each day? What is the point of anyone waking up just to be miserable, go about their business, and go to sleep? Just so they can say they got through another miserable day?

The conclusion seems obvious. One should perish so that the rest can be healthy. That's how animals in the wild ensure the highest number of their offspring end up living. It's the foundation of the predator/prey relationship.

She knows what she has to do, and yet she still has nine decades of worries keeping her stuck in inaction. What would her parents think of what she is going to do? What would Elaine say? What would God think? If the history of the world somehow continued after there was no one around to document it, would she be remembered as a savior to the remaining few, or as the world's last murderer?

She is standing over Justin's bed. The very last Block of the night. Justin, who has never hurt anyone, neither physically nor emotionally. Justin, who from the first day of his existence to his last, has been quiet and motionless. Justin, who Elaine once said was a mountain climber, the final person ever to reach the summit of Mount Everest. He would have stayed on top of the mountain and looked down at the rest of the world for the remainder of his life if he could have. If the weather had allowed it. When you are on top of that mountain, looking out at the expanse of the world, the blur of black earth and white snow mixing everywhere, only the cold and the lack of oxygen can force you away.

"The only reason he had come back down," Elaine had said, "was that it was simply too cold to live up there. So he surrendered to his own limits and returned to join the rest of humanity in their final days. And now, here he is, with us."

Morgan takes the tube leading from Justin's nutrient bag between her index finger and her thumb. Without another thought, she pulls and the tube disconnects from the nutrient bag. Drops of a gelatinous goo drip onto the ground next to Justin's cot. It has no smell. Or maybe it does and she simply can't smell it anymore.

His arms, strong enough to pull him up the sides of mountains, do not push her away. The vice-like grip of his fingers, carved from clinging to rocks all of his life, does not encircle her wrist and beg her to stop what she is doing.

Another drip of the nutrient bag hits the floor. She closes her eyes.

His bag was almost empty anyway. There won't be much to clean up the following day.

Justin is weak as it is, as are all the bodies around her. Without food and water, he won't last more than a few hours.

It's the only way, she tries to convince herself.

The thought is meant to comfort her. The only way she can ensure the health of everyone else, including herself, is if she has fewer people to care for. She simply has too many people to clean and feed and reposition.

There is no reconciling what she has done, though. She keeps expecting Justin to beg for his life, expects him to plead for someone else to die in his place. He could tell her that if this is about survival of the fittest, there are many Blocks who aren't as healthy as he is. He could say that the final person to conquer Mount Everest certainly deserves a better ending than being left for dead in front of all of his neighbors. He says none of this, though. He says nothing at all.

Slowly, she makes her way back to her desk, flips each light switch.

It's the only way, she tells herself.

It's the only way.

The factory goes dark for the evening.

It's the only way.

Outside, a bird chirps, oblivious to the suffering within the walls it craps on each day.

It's the only way.

12

Justin is dead when she checks on him the next day. His lips are grey, his fingers slightly curled. The glossy shine to his skin, that everyone has in the humid Miami weather, is gone. In death, his skin resembles clay more than it does the flesh that used to be there.

His body is removed the same way Elaine's was: with the forklift. The machine picks up the whole package—bed and body and dirty sheets—and hauls them outside to the industrial-sized incinerator.

On its way there, the forklift rumbles over knee-high weeds, shakes back and forth over potholes and cracks in the pavement. A pavement she can no longer see because everything is covered with prickly grass, dandelions, and leaves, a jungle that reaches up to the forklift's tires.

It has been done this way for years. Even when there were ten caretakers left, six women and four men, they were incapable of carrying the bodies. The forklift is a necessity.

Indeed, the machine would make many of her other daily chores easier if she were willing to use it for those purposes. It could help in flipping each Block over. It could carry boxes of nutrient bags and dirty diapers. But she knows the more she uses the forklift the sooner it has a chance to break down, and without it she would have no way to transport the dead out of the building, so she doesn't tempt fate by using it more than she absolutely has to.

She learned valuable lessons from watching George operate the machine. Mainly: always take an extra minute to get the forklift into position. Of course, there was the final Block he tried to carry away, which had fallen to the ground, its skull sounding like a baseball being dropped onto a sidewalk from three stories above. But even before George's eyesight had failed him, the man had always been impatient to get the job done. How many times had she and Elaine watched as the forklift rammed its arms under the bed, hoisted it up, and then watched as the bed teetered to one side? Instead of finishing his job quickly, George had to lower the bed back to ground, reposition the forklift, and try and try again. The dead bodies jiggled like unenthusiastic dancers as the forklift lurched back and forth. It wasn't something you could easily forget.

George never failed to let out a string of curses. Elaine acted like she wasn't paying attention. Morgan, every time she saw the scene unfold, would want to start crying. Why couldn't George realize the bodies were already dead, that it didn't matter how quickly they were removed from the building?

And so Morgan takes her time when she is the one operating the forklift. With her behind the controls, the metal arms pick up the bed, Justin's body still atop it, and carry it across the facility. The other Blocks offer a moment of silence. One of their own has fallen. It is a solemn occasion.

At the incinerator, she pulls a lever and watches the bed rise to the same elevation as the incinerator's feeder. Once in position, she moves the forklift closer. The bed and the body are both consumed in fire.

The body is engulfed in flames, quickly turns to ash. The bed takes much longer. She gives thought to standing near the incinerator as the bed's metal frame melts away to nothing, the body already gone, but she cannot do this. She cannot bear to see a spider missing one of its legs or a common housefly stumbling around with only one wing; there is no way she can stay near the flames as they erase something, even a piece of furniture, because it was home to a life she was supposed to protect.

There are sixty-three Blocks now. The result is a facility with perfect rows and aisles, the cots all perfectly lined up, but with one bed missing at the end of quadrant 4. Now that Justin is gone, she wishes she could forget about the life Elaine had created for him. This act she had to perform would have been easier, somehow, if he had been a shell of a person rather than a great mountaineer. Could she send a mannequin to the inferno? Easily. Could she send Reinhold Messner? No chance.

She wishes the voice Elaine had created for him—crisp and clear, nothing mumbled, everything spoken with an intensity—could be quieted, that the things she spoke of on his behalf—unimaginable determination to get where he wanted to go, the breathtaking view once you get there—could be forgotten. These thoughts plague her and she completes her chores.

Maybe life is measured by the first time you have to hurt another living thing and by the moment you can finally live in peace.

She is exhausted and falls into bed. The gymnasium is dark. The moon offers little illumination. Only the faint outline of objects around the group home can be made out. The shapes of each cot can be seen. Each Block fades into the mass of shadows, though. For once, it is not raining. Also, she notices, for once in a long time her hands do not ache.

There is no noise except for the air conditioner clicking on every once in a while to save them from the hot nights. The birds, wherever they go when the sun is gone, are quiet. The feral cat that calls out in the night—she still can't decide if the calls are to search for a mate or if the cat is scared and alone—is also quiet.

In that moment, she is sure she is being watched. The

hairs on the back of her neck tell her this. They stick straight out. She has goose bumps. There is no noise to indicate she is being spied on. No footsteps. No opening and closing of a door. But the hairs on the back of her neck do not lie. They didn't lie back when she was a young girl watching horror movies, knowing a knife-wielding madman was about to jump out from the shadows and slash a victim to pieces, and they don't lie now.

She looks toward the main entrance. An old EXIT sign, somehow still working after all these years, offers a reminder of the safety precautions that former generations needed. The red glow of the light illuminates almost nothing. No one is there. She looks to the side door, thought of as the emergency exit. Unlike the other one, the sign above this door has long since burned out. But with the moon's light, she can see that no one is standing there either.

I'm going crazy, she thinks. *There isn't even anyone around to spy on me.*

But the feeling does not go away. In fact, it only intensifies. Somewhere, somebody in the enlarged room is staring at her. She is sure of it. Squinting, it looks as though the far corners of the gym are motionless. Each one has the same boxes of supplies that have always been there. She even looks up to the rafters, where the moon comes through, with the thought that perhaps someone is up there. Maybe someone crept in through one of the windows and is sneaking around above her.

What am I doing? I'm alone. If anyone were here, they would have to be a hundred years old. They aren't going to be sneaking around forty feet in the air.

But the feeling of being watched refuses to go away.

After scanning the entrances and rafters, every corner and shadow in the gym, she knows the staring can only be coming from one place. One of the Blocks is staring at her. At least one of them, maybe more.

It's crazy. It's impossible. She knows this. But at the same time, she knows if someone is watching her, it must be someone within the four quadrants. Her eyes scan from bed to bed, but even the closest cots are covered in shadow, the Blocks on top of them vague shapes without distinguishable facial features.

The Blocks can only stare at the things their eyes happen to be resting on, and even then they don't perceive what their eyes are gazing at. But somehow, somewhere, one of them is staring at her. A set of eyes is hunting her. She can feel them casting judgment. The verdict is not good. She feels, from within the dark, hatred directed at her. A plan for revenge is being set.

She wants to call out to whoever is watching. "You there, whoever you are, you don't know what's going on. Let me explain. I'm trying my best."

Right then, her eyes open and she realizes it was only a dream. She was so tired she doesn't even remember closing her eyes, only falling into bed. But as she lies there, eager for more sleep before she has to begin the day's chores, she thinks about the response she might have gotten if the dream had lasted another minute.

Would someone have answered her, confirmed her suspicions that she was hated? But she also has the creeping suspicion that she wouldn't have been able to utter the words she thought to call out. She would have been frozen in place, unable to offer a plea on her own behalf. Instead, her chest would feel like it was weighed down from within. She would be choking on her own silence, helpless.

And that thought, even though the dream is over, makes her shiver. Pulling the sheets tightly around her does no good. Her heart is racing. Perhaps to defy the feeling she had that she wouldn't be able to speak, she takes rapid, quick breaths before declaring to everyone in the gym: "The start of another beautiful day!"

"It's the middle of the night!" Cindy calls out in response. "Shut up."

It turns out that not even a comedian has a sense of humor when everyone should be asleep.

The sun has not yet risen. The clock tells her it won't rise for many more hours. But the more she talks, the more she can believe it really is the start of another brand new and cheery day. And with that, she gets out of bed and begins her chores.

13

It doesn't matter that there is one less Block, Morgan is still nowhere close to finishing before midnight. And every day, she becomes a little slower.

There is only one thing to be done: another body must go so the rest can survive. One less body to clean and feed and reposition means more time for her to sleep and gather her strength. Without rest, she isn't healthy. If she isn't healthy, no one else is either.

Is this what her life has come to—killing a living, breathing person each time she is overcome, overburdened? If she lets someone die today, how long will it be until she has to let another go? Letting one more person die won't put her anywhere closer to being able to care for the rest. All it means is that the remainder of her existence will be marked by how frequently she must go through this.

The thought disgusts her, but at the same time she knows there are no other options. She can refuse to take part in the killings but then every single person in her care begins to suffer. She can sacrifice herself instead of a Block, but it means the rest of the gym's population, whose health and well-being are tied to her own, die a day or two later anyway.

This is the only way.

She looks down at her Jedi, whom she has named

Alokin. Although Alokin was Morgan's idea, the Jedi became Elaine's favorite Block creation that either of them came up with. He doesn't have a lightsaber. He doesn't have control over the Force. In fact, he is nothing but a normal guy. Maybe that is what Elaine loved about their "Jedi Master."

For almost as long as Star Wars existed, people thought it was funny to mark their religion in census reports as being a Jedi. In some countries, Jedi made up as much as two percent of the official population. Maybe one or two of these people really thought they could perform Jedi mind tricks, but everyone else simply liked being part of the phenomenon. A census was conducted five years after the Great De-evolution began. Instead of two percent of the population listing themselves as Jedi, seven percent of people marked that box. Ten years later, in the final census ever conducted, twenty percent of the country listed their religion as Jedi.

Alokin was one of these people.

Elaine had burst out laughing the first time Morgan declared the body in row 1 of quadrant 4 was a Jedi. She had only seen the Star Wars movies once, at a boy's birthday party in elementary school, and they hadn't seemed like anything special, so she wasn't sure where the inspiration came from for this Block to suddenly become the next Obi-Wan Kenobi. Nevertheless, she had found herself going home and testing whether her outstretched arm could somehow make a pencil fly across the room. She still remembers her embarrassed reaction, as a little girl, when nothing in her room moved just because she motioned her hand toward it: "This is so lame!" That had been the end of that.

Looking down at Alokin lying in his bed, she realizes she never told anyone how she tried harnessing the power of the Force in her bedroom. And she realizes the inspiration for the story of Alokin's life was the same thing that made her sit there and test whether she might be able to control objects with her mind: both of them, herself as a little girl and this motionless body next to her in a cot, had just wanted something to believe in. Everyone wants something miraculous to have faith in.

That may have been why people all over the country, people who had never identified themselves as belonging to a specific religion before, gravitated toward being Jedi. They wanted something, at the end, to believe in, even if it just meant believing in the fond memories of being a kid, reminiscing about the things that captured their imagination, allowing themselves to be in awe once more.

It has been many decades since she thought about herself back then. How innocent and naïve she had been! Knowing what she's about to do, the memory of commanding a remote control to fly across the room is one thing she wishes she could now forget. That little girl, who once believed that anything in a movie might be possible, must now admit the extent of her limitations and the effect that will have.

"It's okay," Alokin says. "If you strike me down, I will become more powerful than you can ever imagine."

"I'm not in the mood for that tonight," she says. Then, feeling bad about scolding him near the end, adds, "But may the Force be with you anyway."

And with that, she disconnects his nutrient bag from the tube running into his arm. Her Jedi will be dead tomorrow.

She cannot stop there, though. Sixty-two bodies is still only a little difference. A long, deep breath goes into her lungs, fills her up. That is all of the pause she can allow herself before her next action, which is to walk down row 4 of quadrant 3 and unplug all four blocks there, too.

Her eyes are closed as she walks back to her bed. Tears are already falling down both cheeks. She does not wipe them away. Her hands are shaking uncontrollably at what she has done. But now, finally, she has a chance to finish her chores each day without driving herself until she drops dead. Maybe now she can finish her rounds before midnight and get enough sleep so that the next day seems reasonable.

Maybe.

There were a plethora of movies available to her as she grew up, movies in which a jaded, former professional killer or a still-working hitman confesses that the first kill is the hardest. After that, they all agree that you become accustomed to it; killing becomes easier each time you do it. She knows now that this is not true. There is no way this could ever become easier. She hates herself this time just as much she did the first time.

A list of hopes goes through her head in a cycle: *Please, let God understand why I'm doing this*; and, *Please, don't let there be a God if he sends all murderers to hell*; and, *Please, let something happen so I don't have to keep doing this.*

They are the same thoughts she has the next evening when she makes her way to row 1 of quadrant 4 and to Alokin's bed. He, along with all the Blocks in the back row of quadrant 3, have passed away. The forklift roars to life again. On the way to the incinerator, she finds herself resenting anyone, even an actor playing a role, who tells her it gets easier to kill the more you do it.

It does not get easier.

14

With fewer bodies to care for, she finds herself focusing less on her immediate situation and has more time to think about how she has arrived at this point.

From when she was thirty, when she and her parents arrived in the settlement, to the time she was eighty, there was a steady stream of people migrating south to Miami. New faces would appear at the entrance to the group home. Most of these new arrivals were Blocks, but some were people just like her and Elaine, people who would ask if they could lend a hand. Each new face was a chance for Elaine to tell someone the same old jokes she had told everyone else already and a chance for Morgan to get new suggestions of recipes to experiment with on the food processor.

But the stream of people eventually slowed until it was a trickle, and then, only drops. A single man or woman might appear on the horizon, struggling to make the final mile of their journey on the broken roads. Eventually, even the single new stranger stopped appearing. After that, nature went about its business, making each person a little older every day, sporadically taking someone due to a heart attack or pneumonia.

Not just in her settlement, but in all of them. In addition to the e-mails she wrote to Daniel in Los Angeles, she used to exchange notes with caretakers in New Orleans, Houston, and San Diego. There was a lovely woman working at the San Diego settlement, a West Coast reflection of herself, that Morgan could share all of her sorrows with. This woman, Alaida, had grown up with the same kind of life as Morgan. A life of knowing what it was like to be the only normal child in a room full of children who couldn't talk; years of knowing a different kind of childhood had once been possible but no longer was. This bond united them.

But then, one morning, Alaida's next e-mail wasn't waiting for her. An entire day went by without a message, but Morgan tried to pass this off as the growing responsibilities of a caretaker in the final settlements. She knew how busy she and Elaine were as more caretakers passed away, so she could sympathize with Alaida's tardiness. But no message came the next day either, or the day after that. Alaida had either taken sick and was spending her last days being cared for herself, as she had cared for so many others, or she was already dead. That was the last contact she had with the San Diego settlement. Six months later, Daniel told her that the woman he stayed in contact with from there also stopped e-mailing him, and he assumed the entire settlement was finally gone.

The same thing happened to her friend in Houston. They exchanged messages about what their respective settlements were like, about how the new faces appearing from the north seemed to have finally subsided, and then one day that man also went quiet.

They all did, eventually.

Everyone Morgan has ever known has passed away. With Daniel's death, the Los Angeles settlement is void of human life now, too. She alone is the final person in the world able to form words, capable of articulating her fingers. She alone continues the human lifeline for another day.

This realization does not bewilder her. If anything, she is oddly numb to the fact that she is all that remains. Maybe because she has had a lifetime of endings to prepare for this. Maybe because she is so overwhelmed with her current responsibilities. There is nothing she can do about being the last person other than continue caring for the remaining Blocks in the gymnasium with her. Knowing she is powerless to bring Elaine or Daniel back, helpless in her ability to create new life, allows her to focus on the task of providing for those who cannot provide for themselves.

Their care—the idea that convinces her that what she has had to do to Justin and Alokin and the others is the right thing. As long as she can give these remaining Blocks the best care she is capable of offering, everything else can be forgiven. She forces the thought into her mind, keeps it trapped there, believes it.

In a way, her life is easier with only limited time to contemplate her actions. Hobbling as quickly as she can from bed to bed allows few moments for reflection on the missing row of Blocks in quadrant 3. But it also gives her little time to think of all the things she has lost during her lifetime and little time to assess all the things she has given up to care for others instead of herself. She has lost everything except the actuality of her life. Even her virtue has been lost; she is a murderer.

Her parents are gone. But they would be gone anyway, she tells herself. Everyone's parents have to pass away eventually. However, any other family she could have had is also gone without ever having existed. The man she might have married decided to stay, many decades earlier, when she left with her parents to head south. It hadn't seemed like that big of a deal at the time because Morgan was convinced that if they were meant to be together, life would find a way to reunite them.

Instead, they never spoke again. She thought about calling him or sending an e-mail, but as time went by, she began to question if she hadn't loved him more than he had loved her. Why else wouldn't he contact her? It didn't cross her mind until weeks later that he might have been waiting for the same sign from her. Only then did she realize that she could have made her own fortune instead of relying on the world to determine it for her.

By the time she did call, a year later, there was no answer at his house. Nor did he reply to her e-mail. She used to wonder if he ever got her messages and simply ignored them, spurned by the belief that he must have loved her more than she had loved him, or if he had left her similar messages and wondered why she never replied to them. For a long time after that she tried to picture where he might have spent the remainder of his life, if he lived his final years in a group community, or if he liked being by himself in the forgotten lands that had been abandoned by mankind.

Whereas she is able to create a name and personality and life story for each of her Blocks, she was not able to agree on what might have happened to the young man she loved many decades earlier. He may have only lived another couple of years, or he may have lived to be a hundred. He may have had a completely different sense of humor by the time he passed away; those fifty years in between the last time they saw each other is a long time for someone to change from the person she once knew. It's possible that neither of them would be able to make the other smile anymore. Decades later, she may not even have recognized the man she once loved. That is why she avoids thinking about how he may have died or where he may have spent the remainder of his life. Although she does not try to put together a story for his final years, the one thing she does allow herself is the hope and belief that he thought about her in his last days the way she thinks fondly of him now.

In addition to preventing her from romantic love, the Great De-evolution ensured that any chance she might have had at having children also fell by the wayside. This, at least, is okay with her, though. Growing up during the Great De-evolution, she didn't have the chance to see parents taking their sons and daughters to little league games or to picnics, so it never seemed important to have those same experiences. The charm of having a life growing within her own belly seemed odd because the life she saw all around her was quiet and needed to be cared for. Any appeal at the thought of changing diapers and having someone be dependent on you seemed like an unnecessary burden when she saw Blocks all around her that needed the same thing.

It's not just family, however, that has disappeared from her life. It's also the mundane things, the things she never used to think about. There is no excitement over a new song, movie, book, or TV show, nothing that can take her away, even for five minutes, to another world. The final years of television had nothing but re-runs. It's not fun to turn on a TV when all you see are things that originally aired thirty years earlier.

There aren't even new meals to experiment with on the food processor anymore. At her age, she has had a chance to go through every meal from 001-African Peanut Soup, to meal 999-Ziti. And she has tried every variation for each meal. African Peanut Soup with extra garlic. African Peanut Soup with no chili powder. Ziti with only mozzarella cheese. Ziti with only ricotta cheese. Ziti with only Parmesan cheese. Ziti with all three cheeses. You name it and she has tried it.

With no one else to talk to, she tells her Blocks about the plates of food she makes and then imagines their responses.

"Spaghetti with vodka sauce is pretty gross," she tells the Block who used to be a gardener.

"Why are you telling me? All I get to have is the shit that comes out of this nutrient bag."

The gardener was never very good with people. He was happy when everyone started migrating south because it meant he had entire parks that could be turned into flowerbeds, entire golf courses that could be turned into rose-colored artwork.

It's a shame his family forced him to come down to Miami with them. He has never smiled since then.

She tells a Block who used to be a lifeguard how cream of crab soup is superior to Maryland crab soup.

"Variety is the spice of life," the Block says. "Just

make sure you wait thirty minutes before you go swimming. You don't want to get cramps."

The only people her lifeguard ever had to save from drowning were Blocks who had been left too close to the shore during low tide and were forgotten about by absent-minded family members when the tide started to rise again.

From his peaceful face come the words, "Did I ever tell you about the time I saw dolphins in the water, thought they were sharks, and caused a massive panic?"

She looks at the giant clock on the wall. Even with six of the Blocks gone, she is having trouble keeping the pace she needs.

"I'm sorry. I need to keep moving."

"I understand," he says. "Stay safe."

15

Making her way through the rows of Blocks, she finds herself thinking things like, *I can't believe I ever managed to do this back when there were four entire quadrants; fifty-eight is still too many.*

The first day after an entire row was sacrificed, she was able to finish by midnight. But the next day it was already twenty minutes later before she completed her tasks. Two more days and she was back to one o'clock again.

I'm too old for this. I'll never be able to keep up with all these people.

The thought is still there when she reaches Jeremy, her train conductor. She is only in row 3 of quadrant 2 but is already an hour behind schedule if she wants to be done by midnight.

I do this so everyone else can live, she thinks, her fingers already twisting Jeremy's feed line away from his nutrient bag.

With a click, it disconnects. She lets it fall to the ground. The Block in front of her doesn't reach to reattach the nutrient bag's line. His thick eyebrows don't rise in alarm. He can do nothing but remain staring at her—not at her exactly, but at where she happens to be standing—until she moves along with the rest of her chores and he is staring at the place she used to be. When she comes back the next day, his lifeless eyes will still be fixed on that same spot. That is his life.

She once warned Elaine against personalizing the people in front of them: "You're going to convert this body into a make-believe friend, and one day they're going to die. Isn't it better just to leave them how they are so we aren't as attached when they pass away?"

But her friend had laughed this concern away. "They're already people. We're just giving them memories of a better life than the one they actually had." And then, frowning, "Now stop trying to ruin my game by taking it too seriously."

Jeremy, Elaine had said, was a train conductor until trains became obsolete. There was a brief time, after the migrations started, in which trains were thought to be the savior of the overburdened. It was much easier to load a train with thousands of Blocks and transport them south than it was to load an endless caravan of buses.

The idea did not last long.

Jeremy's life was never the same after the derailment. A train going from Montreal to Boston twisted itself into a fiery ball. Motionless bodies, only a few of which managed to survive, lay scattered about an apple orchard. With the living not being able to yell for help or raise a hand when a call for survivors was made, responders had to walk up to each body and check for a pulse. It took people longer to check for survivors than it had taken to load the train in the first place. In the end, two thousand Blocks, along with the hundred people charged with their care, were dead, their bodies scattered over the distance of a mile.

Someone had inspected the entire line from Montreal to Boston and reported that it was safe. So how did the train derail? Was it sabotaged? Had the inspector simply missed a crack in the iron rails?

Another derailment occurred between Edmonton and Calgary. It was easy enough to get out and change a flat tire if you were driving south and hit a bad stretch of road. The same luxury was not given to the trains; a single problem with the tracks was enough for the entire train to go up in flames. Some said the tracks were being intentionally damaged so the living cargo would have no chance of making the trip safely. Although there was no evidence to support this, no one trusted the tracks after that.

There were people who proposed that the trains crawl along the track while a man walked ahead of it. If the man inspecting the rails noticed a problem, he would signal the train to stop. The journey wouldn't be fast, but unlimited cargo could be transferred with less hassle. This was only attempted once, on the route between Minneapolis and Milwaukee. Somewhere along the way, the man walking ahead of the train was eaten by wolves. No one else was willing to attempt the hike after that.

Everyone else who wanted to migrate south had to use the roads. Giant caravans of buses and minivans appeared on the highways. Train stations around the country were filled with engines and cabooses, each rusting and becoming a home for various species of birds and vermin. All across the country, trains were left in random places on the tracks as if the last conductors had simply disappeared into the wilderness and left the hundred train cars to fend for themselves. Jeremy, Morgan's conductor, had known how to do one thing—get a train from one point to another. After the trains stopped, he had nothing left.

"It'll be okay," she says, putting a hand on Jeremy's forehead. A final gesture of humanity for the man who grew up collecting toy trains, and who, upon seeing one in person for the first time, knew there was nothing else he would rather do with his life.

Jeremy does not focus on what is going to happen to him. All he is capable of is loving his trains: "Do you have any idea what it's like to take hundreds of tons of steel across the country, through mountains, under bridges, across rivers?"

This is exactly the moment she had feared when she told Elaine their game might not be a good idea. She has no idea what Jeremy's parents actually named him. His real name, assuming he had one, disappeared when he was left at the gym's front door. His name, his occupation, even his words, are all thanks to Elaine.

And now Morgan is the one who has to put an end to those memories and experiences. Whether they are real or not does not matter. They are ending all the same. It seems to her that a made-up life should not cause sadness when it's over, especially not compared to the very real lives and memories she shared with Elaine. It does, though. To her, this body in front of her really was a train conductor at one time.

In this moment, she is all too aware of being the last normal human on the face of the earth. Her body offers reminders that she has far surpassed even the most generous life expectancy. These realizations force her to live with the manufactured personalities and histories around her. Only they are here to join her in her final days.

It's obvious that this game makes it even more difficult when she has to sacrifice the good of one for the health of the many, but she cannot help it. Without a bond to keep her thinking each person is an ally in what they are all going through together, she would go crazy. Or she would be like George and simply walk away from the group home one day. But at the same time it destroys her a little when she must do what she does next…

She leaves Jeremy there, the nutrient bag no longer connected to his arm.

"It'll be okay," she says again, this time away from where Jeremy would be able to hear her.

Life is fragile. When he was younger, Jeremy might have lasted a week without having his nutrient bag refilled. Now, his pulse weakens after only three hours. She walks by his bed again once she is done caring for everyone in quadrant 4. When she touches his wrist, she doesn't bother trying to feel a pulse against her fingertips. Her hands have long since succumbed to the trials of old age. Instead, she wants to judge his body temperature. Already, his body is colder than the others. Death is creeping over him.

In the morning, he is even colder. His heart is no longer beating.

She cannot let the body rest amongst the living. Everything she does is guided by the Golden Rule; she would not want to spend the day next to a dead body, so she does not force those in her care, even the voiceless, to suffer through it.

The forklift comes to life. Jeremy's bed, his body still on it, is carried over to the incinerator.

16

It rains all day and all night. At least this time there are no winds, only rain. But the amount of water dropped on top of the group home seems endless.

She was taught in science class that the world has some things that vary wildly based on outside elements: the amount of plant life determines how much oxygen there is, there is a finite amount of gold and silver, the number of mosquitoes fluctuates based on the severity of the previous winter. But for other things, such as energy and water, there is always the same amount. The same quantity of water always exists, just in different forms. A glacier turns to water, the water evaporates but the clouds refill. But if this is true, where is all of this rain coming from?

She still smiles at the thought of her mother walking in on her one evening, after listening to her science teacher talk about how water changes from glaciers to ocean water to rain water and so on in an endless cycle. Morgan had been standing at the bathroom sink with the water running even though she wasn't washing her hands.

"What are you doing?" her mother had asked, her hands on her hips, the pose of an adult ready to put a stop to whatever youthful shenanigans may be going on.

"It's okay, Mom. It just goes into the ground or into

the sewers until it becomes rain again."

Her mother stood in the doorway, her eyes closed, until she could respond without being mean. When she finally did say something, right after reaching over and turning off the water faucet, she had smiled and said, "The amazing things they must be teaching in school these days! It's a shame your science teacher didn't teach you about water bills."

And with that, Morgan had been sent to the kitchen to help clean dishes.

If it keeps raining this way, the entire city will be washed away.

She looks over at one of her Blocks, who promptly says, "If you think this is a lot of rain, you should have seen the concert I played in the Philippines. Now that was a lot of rain."

Jasmine is one of Morgan's favorite Blocks. Inspiration found people in many different ways during the Great De-evolution, but maybe none in such a haunting fashion as Jasmine. In her earlier years, she had been part of a girl band. She and four other girls had hit single after hit single and sold out stadiums all over the country to screaming kids. She tried a similar act, albeit by herself, a couple of years later after the group broke up, but no one in the States seemed to like one girl singing and dancing when there had previously been five. She was hugely popular in Europe and Asia, though. For the next decade, none of her American fans saw her again.

"Great people overseas," she tells Morgan. "It's a shame you never got to go over there."

"Don't rub it in."

"Sorry," Jasmine says. "My bad."

Forgotten in America but as famous as ever overseas, Jasmine continued singing to crowds that could tell she meant everything she said in her songs. When the Great De-evolution began, a new song started playing back home, different from anything she had done previously. It had a ghostly piano, only a couple of notes, accompanied by what sounded like an opera singer bellowing about broken hearts and lost loves. The song reminded everyone of all the people they had ever known that they might never see again. The most requested song in the country, it brought about another round of fame for Jasmine in America.

Sometimes, when Elaine was tired of hearing the rain fall, she would sing a couple of lines from one of Jasmine's songs. Now that her friend is gone, Morgan finds herself humming the lyrics, too:

> *Saw him every day of my life*
> *Until one day he wasn't there,*
> *Guess he made up his mind, just like all the others*
> *If I go south too, will he even care?*

Jasmine had a song for every part of the Great De-evolution that could upset a lovesick teenager. Any time a boy or girl had to say goodbye to their first love because their parents said it was time to move south, they could listen to one of Jasmine's songs and cry themselves to sleep.

> *What's the point of being sad today*
> *When the world will be different tomorrow?*
> *When the world keeps changing every day*
> *Maybe everything can turn out to be okay.*

When people wanted to remember the good times, they listened to her song about how everyone's parents want a better life for their kids. When someone wanted to take their mind away from being scared about the future, they listened to her song about how tragedy spawns the greatest loves mankind can ever know.

And now, finally silent after years of singing, of bringing people to tears with nothing more than her voice, she joins Morgan's other Blocks in quadrant 3.

Jasmine offers the best encouragement she can muster: "I wrote the lyrics to *When the Lights Go Out* during a rain storm just like this one. I always found it inspiring to listen to the rain fall."

"Thanks. I'll keep that in mind."

Morgan finishes cleaning the retired singer, reconnects the nutrient bag to the line running into her arm, makes her way to the next bed. Jasmine will live another day.

But while it rains through the rest of the night without pause, Morgan is unable to find anything thrilling about massive floods that threaten to wash them right out of the only place they can all live together. Humming another of Jasmine's songs provides little comfort.

17

Although she has assigned lives, accomplishments, and personalities to each of her Blocks, made them into complete people, reality always defeats imagination when she tries the same for herself.

She tries to envision herself, not as an old woman alone in Miami, but as a young British nurse. She is in Dunkirk, taking care of scores of soldiers while waiting for the evacuation. The boats never arrive, though. She is Mother Teresa, caring for India's sick and poor. However, Mother Teresa never had to sacrifice one of the wretched for the greater good. She places herself in a science fiction novel, Arthur C. Clarke's last work, unfinished before he died. She and the people she cares for are stationed on a remote moon base, isolated from the rest of mankind. That is why she cannot leave the room with her Blocks. Try as she might, she is unable to forget she is in the remnants of a gutted gym, not a far-away crater.

Every fantasy has a problem. The historical, the pure fiction, it doesn't matter. They are all counterfeit and, eventually, begin to unravel. And each time her daydreams collide with her real life, she is left worse off than before because she realizes her circumstances will never improve. They cannot be altered, can only get worse.

As a nurse, waiting for Churchill's boats to arrive and save them, she cares for the wounded. "I'll get you home safely," she tells one. "Don't worry, the allies will regroup and defeat Hitler," she tells another. She calls her Blocks sir, salutes them, pretends their frail bodies are the result of limited rations or injuries in the trenches. The thunder above her is not thunder at all, but German shells bombarding their encampment.

Although she sometimes feels silly putting on this act, it adds a little excitement to a day's worth of chores. Not a single soldier goes unattended. Each will be cleaned and cared for as if the soldiers' loved ones were right there doing the nursing.

But in the morning, exhausted after a day of ensuring there are no more casualties, of putting her head down each time a bomb goes off overhead, she looks around and sees the same track and field banners hanging above her that have always been there. The banners are covered with a lifetime of dust, are barely legible, yet they still hang overhead to remind her of what high schoolers used to do with their time. Some of the felt letters are missing. A random R, a misplaced C. She finds them, periodically, after they have fallen from the banner and drifted down to the floor. Although not a historian, she can guarantee none of the soldiers at Dunkirk ever looked up and saw a banner declaring who the state champion was in track and field.

In one corner of the group home, parts of the old factory line are pushed into a pile, a reminder of when hundreds of men and women constructed food processors here. Maybe, if she squints her eyes, the scrap metal can be confused for mortars or spare parts for a tank. It always seems to look like remnants of a factory, though.

To add to this, there are no other nurses. Nor does she see soldiers coming and going, checking on their friends periodically in-between preparing for the retreat. Boats never arrive. The storm passes; the blitzkrieg is gone for one more night. The Germans have stopped firing on them for a while.

She is returned to the only life she has for herself. History will not remember her as gallant. Sore, she pushes herself out of bed and begins caring for the Blocks as nothing more than an old woman who has outlived everyone else.

It's no more useful to envision herself as Mother Teresa, caring for the poor and the sick. Like those near death, her Blocks do not cry for help. They do not ask for anything. But while she is old and unbelievably wrinkled—that much of the alternate life is easy to believe—she lacks any kind of faith. She cannot, in good conscience, tell her sick and dying that God loves them, that they will soon be in heaven where they will never feel pain again, because she doesn't know if this is true or not.

A wet compress is wiped across a Block's head as the air conditioning struggles to keep the enormous room comfortable. She offers little affirmations of love in each person's ear. Little additions to her care, such as wet cloths, whispers of love, gently rubbing their hands, only put her behind schedule. She tries not to notice the day slipping away just because she is offering love to each person. For a few hours, nothing is more important than feeling as if each Block is not only being cared for, but is receiving true compassion.

Occasionally, she offers them prayers. But doing so immediately makes her feel guilty because she isn't sure what she believes and what she doesn't. She has no idea what lies in store for her or anyone else. How, then, is she supposed to help make them feel like they are getting ready to pass into the next world? She doesn't even know what she thinks will happen when she dies, so telling them they will soon be reunited with loved ones leaves her feeling like an imposter. She finds herself apologizing for the prayers she offers, as if no prayer at all is better than one that has skepticism behind it.

She is sure Mother Teresa never apologized for one of her blessings. No matter what Mother Teresa believed, her words meant more than anything Morgan can say simply because there was conviction behind them.

The days she is on a remote moon base, she can create a world without being bothered by history or by real-life humanitarians. Sometimes, her spaceship is quarantined from the main outpost. Other times, she is the only survivor after an asteroid has exploded into the mother ship.

Just because the Great De-evolution ended life on her own planet doesn't mean life has to stop all together. Other planets have been colonized. Astronauts are beginning to explore past the Milky Way. Sure, she and the injured astronauts she cares for will eventually meet their end, either after running out of oxygen, getting too close to the sun, or some other routine ending for unlucky space explorers, but at least man has established bases on Mars, on the moon, and will continue to spread out amongst the stars. Mankind will reach out and live on planets that were inconceivable during Morgan's childhood.

But she looks at her laptop, unused since Daniel's death, and knows no one else is out there. Not on the moon, not on Mars. Especially not on Earth. Instead of flourishing, mankind is on the verge of extinction. There is nothing to explore and no one to explore it.

It is painful each time she realizes there is no other reality for her than the one she is in. She is old. She is caring for the last Blocks. That is all there is. As she makes her way through her rounds, refilling each Block's nutrient bag, tears drip onto her shirt and then onto the floor. This is not acknowledged. Instead, she goes on caring for each person as if she isn't crying at all.

Maybe life starts the first time you play make-believe and ends the moment you admit you can no longer imagine something better for yourself than what you have.

18

It's still well past midnight by the time she finishes caring for the Blocks in quadrant 4. There is one bed missing from quadrant 2, four from quadrant 3, and two from quadrant 4, but she has not made up many minutes. Any time gained from having one less Block to care for is lost, the very next day, in the time it takes to power up the forklift, drive it into place, and carry everything to the fires. It's a losing battle.

Her legs feel like they have finished a marathon. Her hands feel like they have broken stone all day at a quarry. And yet all she has done is hobbled from bed to bed and offered basic care to those who need it. She needs more rest than she is getting. Used to being hunched over beds all day, her back refuses to let her stand up straight. Even her fingers betray her. After a day of refilling nutrient bags, pushing Blocks into new positions, wiping bodies down with washrags, her fingers seize up. Some don't move again, no matter how much she rubs them, until she soaks them in warm water.

Sacrificing some of the people she was supposed to be caring for has accomplished nothing.

This thought stays in her head as she lies on her cot before sleeping. Like those all around the gym, her body is perfectly still. If someone else were alive and happened to walk into the gymnasium, they wouldn't be able to distinguish the caretaker from the Blocks until she spoke or until they noticed she was the only one without a nutrient bag.

Her mind is almost never as exhausted as her body, which is unfortunate. If it were, she could go to sleep at night, too tired to worry about the next day and the days after that. Instead, with a body that refuses to move, but a mind that races, she is trapped on her bed, forced to think of how things will play out. She envisions herself killing another Block every day until she is left with one or two people. She imagines herself as the final murderer the world would ever know.

A swirl of life's questions keep her trying to figure things out before it's too late. Is there a God? If there is, what is he thinking as he looks down upon her? Are her actions understandable, given her situation? Or is there no excuse for the things she has done? Is there life after death? If there is, what form does it take? Not just for her, but for her Blocks as well. If there is a heaven, there must also be a hell. Is that where she will spend eternity for what she has done? If it was up to her Sunday school teacher, most certainly. If there isn't heaven, what is there? Is there anything at all, or just nothingness?

She has been told all of her life that murderers go to hell, that only God has the right to take a life. Kill someone: hell. Help someone die: hell. Suicide: hell. Only God can inflict suffering and death as he sees fit. But what she witnesses with her own eyes tells her something different.

She sees life that cannot sustain itself. She sees how an entire group home would be living in misery and filth, each body covered in flies and maggots, if she tried to care for the entire population. It's only when she has slightly more manageable numbers that everyone can live without infections and sores, can have clean clothes. The death of a few pays for the well-being of the many. Somehow, she doubts her Sunday school teacher would have approved of this scenario.

Maybe it's a test. Maybe God really is the only one with the right to take away the life he has created, and this is the apple she has been told not to eat. Well, if that's the case, she is eating every bite and asking for more.

Will she go through all of this just to spend eternity in hell? What would be the point of suffering in this life if she's just going to suffer in the next as well? What was the point of creating Blocks? What was God's reason for turning mankind into a motionless mirror of what it had been? Surely, if God is omniscient, he had to know there would be a point when the last regular people would be overburdened with the task of caring for the silent masses. Is this what he wanted, is it his will?

It's easier to believe there is no God at all. No one is looking down upon her. There is no heaven and there is no hell. She will not spend eternity in fire because she did what she thought was best for her people. Her Sunday school teacher, if he were around, would smack her wrist with a wooden ruler for these ideas. Thankfully, he is not around.

Murderers do not go to hell, and saints do not go to heaven. She will end up in the same place as everyone else— people who have killed others, people who have killed themselves, and people who never killed anyone or anything. Suffering happens because the world is filled with death and pain and agony, not because of a plan from higher up.

As a six-year old girl, she watched a nature show on TV in which the narrator said half of all wild animals in Africa die in their first year of life. Some starve to death. Others are eaten. Some have disease. Some are killed for no better reason than there were people who could kill them. Half of all life. She watched a little cheetah cub die of starvation. She saw a lion cub die by itself in the brush, calling out for its mom. One clip showed a baby rhino being carried away in the jaws of a tiger. *Oh my God*, she had thought. That one show, even for a six-year old, was enough for her to question how there could be a God.

It's not something she likes, this killing of Blocks. But

it's necessary. Doctors didn't operate on patients because they liked cutting people; rather, they liked healing them. This, she tries to believe, is why it's okay to have already sacrificed some of her Blocks and why it will be okay to sacrifice more. She is not being tested, she is just getting by as best as she can, just like everyone else before her got along as best as they knew how.

God did not turn people into Blocks. God did not cause the Great De-evolution. It just happened.

As if remembering her Sunday school teacher, she rubs her wrists. Both hands would be bloody and swollen if that old bastard were here and knew what Morgan was thinking.

She can't help but think, though, if there is no hell for her to rot in, if all people, killers and normal people alike, end up in the same place, what place is it? Is it a mix of heaven and hell? Is it just like this life, only another continuation of it? Or will everyone be reincarnated as various animals, half of which will die within a year of their birth? What's the point of all of this suffering?

Her Zen master Block calls out from across the gym, "Your brain betrays you. It tells you that you were born and that you will die, but this is not true; you are eternal. You have always been here and you will always be here."

She does not know what to say to this, and so she says nothing.

Sometimes she is able to fall asleep feeling as though she has the answers to all of the questions that trouble her. Following the rare day in which she has time to watch the sun set and is well-rested enough the next morning to also see the sun rise, she is sure there must be a God, and a glorious God at that. The days she watches a Block turn to ash in the incinerator, she still thinks there could be a God, but he is vengeful and cruel. If she happens to remember something pleasant from her childhood, only to look up and see a Block's gaze coincidentally focused upon her, sharing in her happiness, she thinks they are alone in the universe. She is fine without a God. When she comes back from the incinerator, the smell of the metal bed frame sending a bitter chemical stench through the air, she feels accused and guilty if that same Block from earlier is staring at her. This is when she wishes she did believe in something greater than herself.

But each time she is sure that one of these possibilities could be the correct one, the following day she wakes up doubting her conclusion. What she thinks most often is that God, if there is a God, does look down on her. And he's not happy at what he sees. She has been told that God has a master plan for everything, but if God's plan is for her to be surrounded by dozens of suffering bodies as they all slowly die together, herself included, she wants no part of it.

How could the God that created the beauty and splendor of the world allow everything to end this way, unless he is spiteful? He would put her in this position, cause this much suffering, just because he can? Nonsense. If that's the case, she is better without God.

She is reminded of the things her priests used to say when she was a child, all of them expecting her to believe what they said just because they were saying it. They had been told the same things when they were young, a pattern that had played out for centuries. But just because something is repeated for a long time doesn't make it true. Mere repetition determined what those men believed. Nothing else.

She needs something more than that.

What she thinks is, if there is a God, he doesn't send you to hell if you commit suicide or if you don't go to church. A God capable of creating our world would not be petty enough to send you to an eternity of flames just because you didn't praise him enough. She believes God couldn't care less if you believe in him or not. God doesn't care which religion you follow. All God cares about is that you try to have a good life, be nice to the people around you, and maybe appreciate the beauty that surrounds us all. Enjoy life as much as you can.

There are also times when she doesn't believe in a

God at all, but more of a cosmic energy that controls all living things. Of course, this is what some people think God is, not a white guy with a white beard and white robes, but the energy that controls and binds all things. This is a nice thing to think about.

She learned in high school that although the universe is always expanding, it always has the same amount of energy. It's just that the energy changes from one form to another, both on earth and on the cosmic scale. A tree dies. The energy it had goes away from it, but is not gone. It transfers to the grass and plants around it. A star gives warmth to a series of planets, only to explode in a supernova. And all of that energy disperses throughout the galaxy. She thinks of an ant dying and how its body provides the ground with nutrients that the grass needs, which in turn feeds the animals that need to eat grass for their own life. And because energy is always around us in one form or another, always recycling itself, she believes there is something after all to this cosmic energy idea.

The thought helps her feel like this is not the end, but only a transition from one phase to another. There won't be a traditional heaven or hell, but those places always seemed a little too human for her—places created by the limitations of the men who wrote them into the Bible, not a place that a god capable of creating our world and the life in it would actually make.

If there is an afterlife, she wonders how the Blocks will get along in it. Will they be normal then or will they continue to be motionless and quiet? Is their current condition only temporary until they pass on? She likes this as her final thought before she closes her eyes because it allows her to imagine Jeremy and Alokin and Justin finally having a chance to express themselves, to know love, to be happy.

19

Each night, she wakes from dreams that leave her filled with dread. Most nights she cannot remember what the dreams were about. She wakes clutching the blanket over her as if it will protect her. Sometimes, she is gasping for air as though she had been holding her breath in her nightmare and that made her hold it in real life too. Each morning, she awakens to feelings of being hunted, scared, unsettled. Her eyes scan the group home for anything that could be creeping up on her, a threat she has not thought of. Maybe her subconscious is trying to warn her of something.

Maybe, she thinks, her subconscious is trying to tell her to stop killing Blocks.

During her chores, she pauses alongside Cindy, the comedian, in hopes of hearing something funny. If anyone is able to make her smile after a night of unrest, it's the woman who toured the final settlements, making everyone laugh and, miraculously, allowing people to forget the end of man was approaching. But there is no joy to be found today. Cindy's perpetually happy face, a face that could have told a lifetime of jokes if circumstances were just a little different, still stares up toward Morgan, but there is no good humor today.

"Sorry," Cindy says, her beautiful blue eyes as large as ever, "even comedians need a break from joke-telling every once in a while."

Morgan looks at the over-sized clock on the wall, a remnant of the days when boys and girls, ages 13-17, had gym class in this very spot. At her current pace, she won't finish her chores until after midnight again.

Better to get this over with quickly, she thinks, before twisting the nutrient bag's connector counterclockwise. Cindy's nutrient bag is no longer feeding into the clear tube that runs into her arm. The nourishment the comedian needs to continue telling jokes is withheld.

"Is this because I wouldn't tell you a god damned joke? Is this what I get for being serious?"

Morgan ignores the outburst and walks away.

Even with eight fewer Blocks to care for, she is not keeping pace. It's past midnight when she finishes, exhausted. A light rain trickles down upon the roof. Without thinking of Cindy, she closes her eyes and is quickly asleep.

But just as quickly, her eyes re-open.

The gymnasium is quiet and dark. The moon shines through the top windows, allowing a gentle wash of yellow light into the living quarters. The outline of each bed is illuminated. The rain has stopped. The giant room is noiseless, yet something has woken her.

Immediately, for a reason she cannot determine, her eyes move to Jimbo, the detective who caught the Block Slasher. Located in quadrant 1, Jimbo is lying on his cot only twenty feet away from where Morgan sleeps. There is no reason to focus her attention on him instead of someone else. Even so, she stares at him as if expecting something.

Without moving, without the slightest motion or even a single word, she continues to look at him. She has been the sole caretaker in the group home for over three weeks now, has not had another living person to speak to within the gymnasium's walls in that time.

And then it happens.

Jimbo's head rolls to the side. Morgan gasps. He is staring straight at her. As impossible as this simple gesture is, she is sure it is not an accident; his head did not just happen to roll to one side, his eyes just coincidentally happening to fall upon her. Against all possibilities, he has turned to face her. And he is not smiling.

In shock, her first instinct is to bring her hand to her mouth. But her hand won't move. Confusion almost outweighs the shock she was just feeling. Maybe her arm fell asleep. If she rubs it with her other hand—but her other hand won't budge either! She cannot move. Not even her fingers will twitch.

Stay calm. Stay calm.

Panicking would be completely understandable. She would not blame herself for screaming. It would be perfectly reasonable, upon seeing a Block turning and staring at her and her realizing she cannot move, for her mind to shut down, for her to black out, maybe even piss herself from pure fright.

Stay calm. Stay calm.

Instead of panicking at her paralysis, though, she forces her mind to think of how this could be happening. Little whispers of fear creep into her head: *what if this isn't temporary, what if she will never be able to move again?* She forces these thoughts away. In their place, she tries to appreciate Jimbo as a silent partner in the ordeal they have been going through.

His eyes tell her he wants no part of being associated with her, though. His eyes show disgust, hatred.

She tries to stay positive, forcing her breathing to remain slow: *Now I know what it's like to be motionless and silent. Now I know what they're going through.*

Jimbo blinks but does nothing else. He does not speak. His narrowed eyes, not wavering from her, stare coldly in her direction, letting her know what he is thinking of saying: "Did it make you feel good to pull the plug on Cindy today? Did you feel good about yourself the other day when you killed Jeremy? Did it make you feel powerful?"

Morgan wants to yell, "Of course not! I didn't want

to, but I had no choice." No words come, though. She is mute.

"You make me sick," Jimbo would say. "I used to arrest freaks like you every day. You're no better than the Slasher."

"No! No!" she wants to scream. "You have it all wrong." But as hard as she tries, she cannot make her tongue move in her mouth, cannot force her throat to push sounds forward. Instead, she remains quiet, motionless, staring back at Jimbo. Sweat forms on her forehead.

"Cat got your tongue?" Jimbo says. "How does it feel knowing you can't defend yourself?"

She wants to explain how awful she feels each time she disconnects a feeding tube. If she walks away without crying, it's only because she needs to keep moving, keep going with her chores without thinking, in order to continue caring for everyone else. But these are things she cannot say.

She feels herself begin to panic, to lose control.

If only she could prop herself on one elbow and explain how she can't even bring herself to kill a spider or a cricket, but that killing one Block made more sense than having all of the rest of them suffer. Surely, even a police detective can understand that. She cannot move, though. Her body is paralyzed. No words are spoken. No defense is offered.

Jimbo's eyes become tiny slits. "How would you like it if I walked up to someone you loved and strangled the life out of them? Would you like that? Would you like to watch as I forced the air out of their body and they died right in front of you?"

"No! Of course not," Morgan wants to say, but she can do nothing but blink.

"I ought to come over there and take away all your food and water. How long do you think you could last if I left you to die? A couple hours? A day? You're old and weak, just like us; it wouldn't take long for you to die. Would you beg me to put you out of your misery?"

"No!" Morgan wants to scream.

"You're lucky I'm not the Slasher. You're lucky I'm not like you."

Finally, her body listens to her. Her eyes open. She bursts up from the bed in a sweat. She is sitting upright, breathing heavy. Sweat runs down her forehead and into her eyes until she wipes it away. In the dark, only the moon offering light, she looks over at Jimbo, whose head is staring up at the ceiling.

The nightmare is over.

Except for the sound of droplets of rain hitting the metal roof, the gym is silent. All of her Blocks are quiet and motionless, the way they always are. Her entire body is trembling. Pulling the blanket over her, rubbing her arms, taking deep breaths—none of it works to calm her down.

The clock says it is only three thirty in the morning. She tries to close her eyes and go back to sleep. It's useless. After a dream like that, she's not even sure she wants to go back to sleep. With a groan, she rolls out of bed and begins performing her chores for the day.

Jimbo's words echo in her head as she splashes cold water on her face and begins shuffling from cot to cot: *"Would you beg me to put you out of your misery? You're lucky I'm not like you."*

20

Cindy, like the others, is dead the next morning. Her mouth is slightly open, stuck in the pose of someone who wanted to say one final thing. Her eyes are open but have no gloss to them. The forklift appears at the comedian's bedside, rumbling and ready to go to work.

Morgan still hears the imaginary words that would be spoken from the bed: "I've heard of comedians being booed off stage, but this is ridiculous!"

As the forklift scoops the bed up, Cindy adds, "And I thought the crowd in Los Angeles was tough. At least they just threw tomatoes at me. Can I please just say one last thing? Yes? Thank you. What do Blocks and the bubonic plague have in common? They both really fucked mankind!"

With Morgan's guidance, the forklift arrives at the incinerator.

"Oh well," the comedian says. "It's been fun."

Morgan can't help but think, as the bed disappears into the flames, that the comedian still had a wry grin on her lips, as if slightly amused by her final exit. Then she is gone and Morgan has one less person to care for as she makes her rounds.

Ever since Elaine created the game of assigning lives and personalities to each Block, Morgan has been around extreme instances of almost every imaginable occupation. Jimbo isn't just a regular police detective, his strict adherence to the letter of the law makes him incredibly gruff: "Like them or not, laws have to be obeyed during the Great De-evolution, just like they had to be obeyed when there were still young punks to arrest." Another example was their brash lawyer, convinced of his own brilliance: "I'll bet you a thousand dollars that I could get a jury to convict a Block of a crime." One was a prodigy on the piano and another was a zookeeper. They had it all.

So many people filled the rows that Elaine and Morgan's imagination couldn't think of additional careers. In these cases, they created different temperaments for the people with duplicate jobs. That was how she had one pilot who was always happy to go into the clouds and another that hated everything about his job. Jimbo, surly as ever, was joined by an introverted detective and also by an alcoholic private investigator. The brash lawyer, located in quadrant 2, was in between a divorced public defender and a corrupt federal judge.

In addition to Leonardo, her famous painter, she also found herself taking care of Nathan. Nathan was her Block who had always dreamed of being a famous artist but never had the belief in himself necessary to pick up a brush. "Maybe tomorrow," he would say while imagining all the things a blank canvas could contain, none of which would ever be turned into reality.

And there was Charlotte, a struggling artist who sold her works on the corner of the street for barely enough money to pay her rent, but who loved painting, knew it was her purpose, and continued on that path her entire life. "I'd rather starve doing what I love than be rich doing what I hate."

And there was Charlie, her artist who was loved for his collection of paintings titled *Block Consciousness*, and who became famous in various art circles for being the final heir to Jackson Pollock. Nobody could figure out what each painting was supposed to be until Charlie provided the title. "Block Horrors" gave viewers an idea of what the swathes of black and red across the tan canvass might represent. "Block Dream" explained why the black canvass had splashes of the entire color spectrum with what might be an eyeball in the very middle.

She has even had the fringes of society in her midst. One of the men who lives in quadrant 4 is an anarchist whose only outlet for expressing himself was various acts of mild mischief, like spray-painting walls with anti-government slogans and putting stickers on street signs. "If you believe what your government tells you, you're a fool!"

A stripper resides in quadrant 1. Her plan was to strip only until she got her degree, but, the only kid in her class without student loans to pay back after she graduated, she realized she would be better off financially if she kept removing her clothes for strangers than if she put her degree to use. That's how she came to spend three decades of her life giving men lap-dances. "It's not the life I imagined for myself, but my Block customers can't move so I don't have to worry about being groped."

Quadrant 3 has her most infamous Block of all. Gault was the world's last evil mastermind.

"Personally, I think you're handling yourself fabulously," he has told her on more than one occasion.

She never knows if he is serious or joking. Maybe he likes being around this lottery of death. Perhaps he is jealous that he isn't the one in charge of deciding who lives and who dies.

He doesn't look like much of a threat to the world— no one does when they are almost a hundred years old—but in his earlier life he made plans to buy enriched uranium from Russian terrorists so he could build a nuclear bomb. When the FBI arrested him—this was around the same time New England and the Northwest states began to migrate south toward the final settlements—they found an apartment full of elaborate schemes to produce mass destruction. Gault had plans to bomb railroad tracks and destroy famous landmarks. He wanted to blow up group homes and contaminate lakes. If it caused wide-spread death and suffering, he wanted it.

Morgan has never asked Gault, and he has never volunteered, how he feels about ending up in one of the very group homes he wanted to destroy. (Elaine was always the one who liked expanding on Gault's life and adding details to what the mad scientist would be thinking.)

The closest he has come to speaking to Morgan was the veiled comment, "It wasn't actually about blowing up this or destroying that, it was about the pandemonium. Nothing is more pure than chaos."

She is pretty sure he lost his mind a long time ago. And yet she never thought to disconnect his nutrient bag before Alokin's or Justin's.

As if sensing this thought, he laughs and says, "Don't try and make sense of madness, my dear. It'll leave you crazy."

Even with all these people and all their roles, there are still a few characters in her life that she has never been able to manufacture amongst her Blocks. None of them are extended members of her family. She had a mother and father. No one in her care can become her make-believe parents. She never had a brother or sister, but she has also never found someone she thought resembled her enough in the group home to play the part. She is kindred spirits with the Block who is still trying to find her place in life. But that Block's long, slender nose and thin, black eyebrows prove there never could have been a blood relation between the two of them, not even as cousins.

Nor has she been able to find a lover amongst the rows of Blocks. Jeremy, from quadrant 2, was certainly handsome enough. Caesar, from quadrant 4, was a great listener. But no matter how becoming or attentive someone is, she knows she cannot put herself in a relationship that doesn't exist. She can assign occupations and personalities, those things are easy, but love should not be on a pretend basis. Love is something that should never be acted out.

Even when she thought about the possibility of one of the Blocks as her lover, she knew it would be a non-physical relationship, and thus, one that would only make her even lonelier by its limitations. Maybe she could give one of the Blocks a kiss on the cheek each night and fantasize about it leading to more. Maybe she could hold a Block's hand while she speaks to them. The word 'love' might be offered in a whisper on the nights when she is lonely and needs someone to comfort her. But anything else is not realistic, and, because of that, can only make her sad. Letting her hand linger on a motionless body would only remind her of how far she has gone from the relationship she had when she was thirty, reminds her of all the ways a real lover could touch her that no one else is capable of now.

She would love, more than anything, to have a partner in all of this. Elaine was her partner in caring for the Blocks, but that's not what she means. Ideally, a real partner would hold her in his arms, lay next to her at night, kiss her awake in the morning. Those are the things she had briefly, when she was thirty. Those are the things she has missed ever since. She can walk up to any cot she wants and say, "I love the way you touched me last night," but the words would only mock her situation. Her evil mastermind, her doctor, the lawyer, the artists, all of them, their lives are the only variety she can have.

Having abandoned the idea of assigning romance to one of her Blocks, she tries to think of one of them as a killer in their midst. She started with sixty-four Blocks. Now, there are only fifty-six. Who amongst them is sneaking through the shadows in the middle of the night to commit murder? Turning the deaths into something more than they are, something nefarious, will surely take her attention away from the desperation of her situation.

There is a problem with this, though. The tiny part in the back of her mind that knows every conversation she has with these Blocks, every personality she and Elaine have handed out, is nothing but a forgery, this part of her understands that if this becomes a case of murder, as opposed to doing what is necessary during hard times, it means that she is not simply a caretaker doing what is best for the entire home, but the final incarnation of Jack the Ripper or the Green River Killer. The little voice in the back of her head does not let her forget that if there is a serial killer, she is it. She would rather not have the excitement of hunting for a murderer if she knows herself to be the culprit.

She can walk up to one of the Blocks and say something like, "I know it was you, just confess!" but at night, with the lights off, in the moments before she goes to sleep, she would know she's no better than the little girl who tried to blame an empty cookie box on her stuffed animals rather than taking the blame for herself.

Her detective would not be of much help. Jimbo would take one look at the case and say, "I don't know how you can think Charlie might be the killer. He has an alibi and he has shown no inclination toward this type of behavior. I'm beginning to suspect your detective skills."

Her lawyer would have to agree. "I don't know of a single prosecutor that could win this case. I smell easy money for the defense."

Neither of them would come right out and say they think she might be the killer, but she can tell they are thinking it.

And the last thing she hears before she goes to sleep is Charlie defending himself: "I have an entire quadrant of Blocks who will vouch for my whereabouts. Do you have anyone who will vouch for yours?"

She has no answer.

21

There are days she thinks God is keeping her alive until she believes in him. Why else has she lived on after everyone else has died? She must live until she understands his master plan for the world, until she grasps her role in that scheme. There are also days she thinks God is keeping her alive until she understands her sin and repents for it. He is giving her time before it's too late. And then there are also days when she doesn't think God cares one way or the other; he just created the universe, he doesn't have a preference as to what she does in these final seconds. There are times she thinks God must regret the blunder of creating man in the first place. If God is the cause of all things, she reasons, the Great De-evolution is his doing as well. He must be biding time until she, the very last person left, goes away to join Adam and Eve and their descendants, all the way up to Morgan's own parents and everyone else who has ever lived.

There are, of course, also many days in which she doesn't think God is out there at all. She was created by an accident of the universe, nothing more. She has no role, no destiny. It is nothing more than a cosmic joke that she is overburdened with the care of too many people. She has no sin to repent, nor does she have to understand a master plan. Everything is mere chance.

This spectrum of beliefs follows her from the time she wakes up until the time she finishes caring for the final quadrant of Blocks. The ideas flow one to the next, merging together, drifting off. During breakfast, she believes God has a purpose for her. While she is caring for the Blocks in quadrants 1 and 2, she is sure that she's alone and that no deity is watching over her. By dinnertime, she is back to thinking there is a God but that he simply doesn't care what happens to her. Except for the Blocks around her, she might as well be alone. By the time she is done cleaning the face of the last Block in quadrant 4 and turns the gymnasium lights off for the night, she thinks her day isn't about sinning or understanding or anything else; it is void of meaning. Or, maybe, it is whatever she makes of it.

She has never bothered McArthur, her Block who suffers through his own religious doubts, with these worries. He has enough to think about each day, about heaven and hell and previous lives and next lives, without being troubled with Morgan's own concerns. She passes by him each day without a single word spoken between them, only an understanding that neither of them knows very much.

Every once in a while, he offers her tidbits of wisdom: "Religion is only flawed because the men who created each religion were flawed," and "Faith is nothing more than knowing there is something greater than ourselves, something we cannot see or understand, but it's out there."

She is never sure if these are arguments for or against one way of thinking. McArthur probably isn't sure either. She wants to ask if he thinks she is being judged for her actions in these final days, or if he thinks God is understanding of what she is going through, but she doesn't ask such questions out loud. He is looking for his own answers. Any response he can offer would be weighed down with doubt.

His cot is between two other people who he has never been able to speak to. His entire life has been spent in a chair or a bed.

Without asking, she knows what he wants to say:

"What kind of God would create a life like mine, a life that can't support itself? Surely not a loving God. But at the same time, nature doesn't create life that can't support itself because that goes against the very nature of evolution and survival of the fittest, so maybe this *is* due to a higher power." He scowls before adding, "So many questions."

Without saying anything, she nods at him as she passes by his bed.

After finishing up at the last cot, she looks back at the rows and rows of people in front of her. Her watch says it's one in the morning. She is losing the battle again. There are eight fewer Blocks in her care today than there were when Elaine died, and yet she is still an hour behind where she used to be.

She looks back at a man named Algernon in row 1 of quadrant 1, the very first Block Elaine ever named. Next to him sits a woman named Paula, one of the first Blocks Morgan gave a name to.

She still remembers the way Elaine's eyes rolled when she said, "I named this one Algernon, and you pick something like Paula for this one?"

Elaine had gone on to say Algernon was a scientist who refused to give up on finding a cure for Blocks. Morgan frowned and said Paula was a scientist who didn't bother trying to find a cure and had moved south before anyone else.

"Are you serious?" Elaine had asked. "You're awful at this game."

As Morgan looks at the two Blocks now, she knows the two bodies are approximately the same age; everyone who was older has already passed away. The same thing goes for Morgan. She was born when 99.9999% of babies were Blocks. She has never met anyone born later. Elaine had been two weeks older. But a common age is all that the two Blocks in front of her share.

She looks at Algernon, then Paula, then back at Algernon. Algernon, with his tiny mouse-like nose and mouth, has the facial features of someone who was never

Chris Dietzel

happy or unhappy, someone who was too determined to waste time with emotion. His strong jawline, his lack of wrinkles, reveal his character. In contrast, Paula has gray hair, some of which refuses to give up the final remnants of the blonde that used to get her so much attention.

Morgan's eyes remain on Algernon. This part, the indecision, is the thing she tries to avoid. Once her mind is made up, she acts. She must move fast or else she second-guesses what she is doing, and that makes it all the worse in the end.

Her fingers twist and disconnect Algernon's feeding tube. Instead of leaving and going back to her own bed, though, she remains there, watching him, holding his hand in her own. Maybe this compassion will help the nightmares go away. Maybe it's her guilty conscience at letting them die alone that causes her so much torment.

The story she learned about him, through Elaine, was that he had been fascinated by science for as long as he could remember. On his seventh birthday, his parents bought him his first telescope. His favorite Transformer had been the one that changed into a microscope. In ninth grade, his science fair project beat the best efforts put forth by all the juniors and seniors.

When the Great De-evolution began, he joined scientists all around the world in trying to formulate a cure for the Blocks. And if not a cure, then at least a vaccine. Decades went by. His colleagues, the greatest minds of medicine, neurology, and biology, passed away or disappeared. He e-mailed a chemical compound formula to a doctor in Sweden only to receive a crudely worded reply, typed by the doctor's assistant, saying her boss had died the night before, at the age of seventy-nine.

He e-mailed a series of chemical compound chains to a doctor in Paris without ever receiving a reply. The doctor, like so many others around the world, disappeared from normal life and became just another nameless person trying to get themselves and their families closer to the equator and to warmer weather. One day, the Parisian doctor had been a Rumford Medal winner and a recipient of the Marcel Benoist Prize, and the next day he was just another old man driving through long stretches of forgotten grape fields on his way to meet family in Spain.

Through it all, Algernon persisted. He was not deterred when his peers passed away. He was not discouraged when they gave up the fight and decided to vanish with their families. Each morning, he sipped a cup of coffee, read the paper, and then went about the business of finding some way to create a baby that could cry, reach for its mother, laugh, learn. Possible cure after possible cure failed. He never would have predicted that one altered protein could cause this whole mess and lead to mankind's end.

A promising experiment to make the protein regenerate itself turned out even worse than the tests he hadn't expected decent results from. But he never gave up. Day after day, year after year, he attempted to save the human race. And while he never did find a cure—no one ever would—he tried and tried until it wasn't humanly possible to try any more.

But, she thinks, still holding his hand, his life wasn't any less meaningful just because a cure wasn't found. He still dedicated himself to something he believed in. That counts for a lot. He still managed to wake up every day and go to sleep every evening with a passion for something. She admires this about him. It is a more respectable life, looking back, than Paula's, who gave up the first time she was overwhelmed and became one of the many people looking out only for herself and for no one else.

Morgan understands now why Elaine had rolled her eyes at the way Paula had supposedly lived her life. Elaine had been right: Morgan wasn't very good at their game.

Algernon's nutrient bag begins to drip onto the floor. Any respect she has given his life is tainted by the groan she lets slip, knowing she will be the one to clean the mess up the next morning.

Drip.

It's always her; there is no one else. And yet she leaves the bag to continue dripping on the floor rather than letting it go into a bucket or onto Algernon's blanket.

Drip.

She leaves Algernon there, cursing herself for letting that thought of inconvenience, the sound of dripping, ruin a memory as pure as someone's life being dedicated and determined.

Maybe the next day will be better. There is always that hope. Even McArthur would have to agree with her on that.

22

A voice echoes across the gymnasium: "Remember what it was like after gym class when you were tired and thirsty?"

Her muscles clench up. Her heart beats so fast she has trouble breathing.

"Remember the way your dry tongue kept sticking to the roof of your mouth?" the voice says. "Remember how good it felt to feel the cold water from the fountain?"

The voice does not have to speak loudly for her to hear it. Even the softest noise echoes from one end of the gutted room to the other. In a different setting, a happier setting, the room would be perfect for an orchestra. Beautiful music would bounce off every wall. Instead, she wishes, as this voice continues to speak, that there were a way to block out what she is hearing.

"You can forget about that water. You're going to know exactly what it's like to feel your body shutting down. Even if I did have extra water, I wouldn't give it to you. I'll pour it on the ground right in front of you and laugh."

She wants to defend herself, wants to yell that torturing her isn't fair, that she is doing the best she can. No sounds will form, though. Her hands are motionless. Her mind screams all the things she wants to say on her behalf, but there is no actual noise.

"Your lips will crack open. You'll feel shooting pains in your stomach. Your throat will burn. How do you think it'll feel to know you're slowly dying? Twenty-four hours doesn't seem like a long time until you're begging for a drop of water every minute. It will feel like an eternity. You know water will never come. You're going to die here, and it's not going to be pretty. I can't wait to see how you suffer."

She feels herself almost lose control of her bladder, knows she is coming very close to pissing herself right where she lay. Ashamed, one of her thoughts is actually that the urine might be the only thing around to keep her hydrated.

The voice bursts into laughter. He, whoever he is, can either sense what she was thinking and takes delight in how hopeless she feels, or else he simply enjoys being able to taunt her for as long as he wants without any protest.

The last thing she hears, before opening her eyes, is, "We'll see how long you can live. You'll be trapped on your bed with all of us looking down at you, and we'll all be laughing at your misery as you beg us to let you die."

Then her eyes open. Gasping for air, she realizes her mouth is completely dry. Her tongue feels like sandpaper until she drinks from the glass of water on her bedside table. The glass is empty after four eager gulps.

During her rounds, she has found herself avoiding eye contact with the Blocks who have appeared in her nightmares. This voice was not distinguished enough, however, to know which of them was taunting her. It could have been any of them. Unsure which man was laughing at the fact that she almost pissed herself, she finds herself hurrying past half the beds. The men still need her care, but she barely touches them, refuses to look at them, repositions them as quickly as possible, refills their nutrient bags as fast as her old hands will allow. She finds herself replaying conversations she has had with each person, trying to think whose voice may have been echoing in her nightmare.

Why does it even matter? It's not like I'm going to let them die just because I had a nightmare about them.

But maybe, she thinks, she can convince them that she is trying her best, that maybe if she speaks to them during the day, when she isn't terrified and can form words, they will understand where she is coming from.

Outside, it rains all day. It was raining when she woke up and it's still raining as she cares for the Blocks in quadrant 3. An amazing amount of water falls on the group home. If it continues to rain like this, the entire facility will be flooded and she won't have to worry about which Blocks are threatening her and which ones are innocent.

Her Zen master is one of the few men who cannot be the culprit. In his soothing voice, he says, "You are not so different from the rest of us and we are not so different from you. Experiences are shared between all of us more than you realize."

"Thank you, Coelho."

But one Block's sympathy does not fool her into thinking the nightmares will stop. The bad dreams occur almost every night now. A few kind words will not change that. Sadly, the frequency of the dreams does not make them less terrifying. No matter how many times she has a nightmare of being motionless and mute, of having the very Blocks she cares for threaten her with death, she always wakes in a sweat or in the middle of screaming the words she is trying, with futility, to bellow.

It is never the same person threatening her, never the same Block two nights in a row who holds a grudge. The variety of the Blocks in her dreams makes her feel like they are all against her. One night the offender will be her detective, another night it will be a former teacher, and yet another night it will be the psychologist. Never the people she has let starve to death. Always the people who still remain. Why is that? If anyone should hold a grudge against her, it should be the people she has sent to the incinerator. She is unable to figure out why the people who should be grateful that they are still receiving care are the ones who torture her, while the dead, who should be seeking vengeance, leave her alone.

Even the Blocks who look like they would never hurt a fly, never want to cause anyone pain, are vicious when she sleeps. There is a very sweet-looking old woman, Rachel, in row 3 of quadrant 3. As a veterinarian, Rachel took care of animals her entire life until she was mauled by a pack of feral Wiener dogs. This was in the middle of North Carolina, where it was reported that packs of wild dogs outnumbered the wolves and bears. It was impossible for her to see these little creatures as anything other than sweet animals. It was her own fault that she thought they wouldn't attack her. The scars on her forearm are probably what made Elaine give her that story.

Although Rachel was permanently scared of dogs after that, she never stopped radiating a love for life in general. She still smiled every time she saw a flock of birds migrating south. She still broke into baby talk every time she saw a cat wandering the streets. Her hazel eyes brightened each time a squirrel saw her and scurried away. She apologized to the flowers before picking them for a vase, and under her watch a spider was ushered outside rather than stepped on.

And yet this same woman appeared in one of the most recent, most murderous dreams that Morgan has had. The nightmare started with Morgan waking from her sleep to the realization that Rachel was staring at her from across the gym. The veins in the veterinarian's hands were bulging. The fingers curled, showing off the long fingernails that would claw into Morgan's throat or maybe tear her tongue right out of her mouth. The look on Rachel's face said she would like nothing more than to rip Morgan's eyes right out of their sockets. That was when Morgan woke, gasping for air and rubbing her eyes.

The nightmares occur on the nights she has unplugged a nutrient bag, but they also occur on the nights she has announced to the entire gym that she will stay awake as long as it takes to care for every last body. It makes no difference. She still wakes gasping for air, her hands reaching for her throat, sure that a murderer's fingers must be ripping her neck apart.

Nothing she does matters anymore. She realizes this now. If she is going to have the dreams anyway, she might as well take another Block to the incinerator.

"What message are you trying to send me?" she asks, looking up at the roof.

No one answers.

But that evening, unable to stay on schedule, already tired and functioning ineffectively from the previous day, she knows there is only one option. One of her painters in quadrant 2 will go. Passing by Leonardo and Charlie, she comes upon Jarrett, who specialized in watercolors. It was obvious, when he arrived at the doorstep of the group home with a finely trimmed moustache and van dyke, that that he must be an artist.

Before the Great De-evolution, Jarrett loved painting landscapes of English cottages and Greek ruins. As mankind began to vanish from the Earth, he started painting scenes of abandoned farms, of caravans traveling south on barren landscapes, of jungle gyms that were rusted and falling apart without children to play on them.

Morgan's hand lingers at the painter's forearm, provides a soft caress, then disconnects his nutrient bag. The last thing he leaves behind, a painting of a deserted city, will be all that remains to mark that he was ever there.

23

Jarrett is dead when she checks on him in the morning. His fingers, which used to hold paintbrushes, now stick together with the first signs of rigor mortis. Of all the bodies she has disconnected from their nutrient bags, not one has struggled to stay alive. She checks on them even before she brushes her teeth or sips her coffee. None of them have been strong enough to fight on into the next day; they are all too eager to leave this place and go to whatever is next.

She takes him to the incinerator before she has breakfast. It's what she would want if she were the previous night's victim. Again, the Golden Rule. Even the killing: yes, she thinks, she would be perfectly willing to be sacrificed for the good of the group if it meant everyone else would stay healthy. Her willingness to be put in their place, in the fire, has become one of the reasons she can justify her actions.

With another bed and body gone, she rushes to eat her breakfast. The cream of wheat and coffee are both produced from the food processor. In these quiet moments she finds herself thinking of everything else she could possibly be doing at the end of her life instead of caring for a giant room full of Blocks.

When she was a little girl, if asked what she would do right before the world ended, she would have said something like, "Get married in Paris to the cutest boy I can find!" This was before she even understood what marriage entailed and before she realized boys' looks were overrated. As a teenager, she probably would have grimaced at the question and replied, "Put on an Elvis Costello CD and watch the world end from my window." As a young woman, she might have said, "Get on a plane and see as many European capitals as I can before it's too late." Now, she might just go outside and wander the empty, overgrown city streets, look at abandoned building after abandoned building, and glance up at the sky and the sun and the clouds, which have stayed exactly the same through the years while everything else has changed.

A sense of guilt immediately invades her each time she lets herself daydream of other ways to spend her time. The Blocks cannot change their situation. None of them would volunteer to be helpless. She knows she shouldn't resent them for how everything is turning out. Her father would be proud of the Catholic guilt he instilled in her. Once it's there, it's almost impossible to get rid of.

Looking around, the aisles of Blocks aren't what they used to be. Justin's cot is gone. So are Alokin's and Algernon's and Jarrett's. An entire row is gone from quadrant 3. Is it possible, she wonders, for someone to see the way things are going and give her credit for trying her hardest, or would they take one look at the blank spaces and accuse her of being a murderer?

She passes by Eduardo, who would have been a world famous soccer player in Europe if the leagues hadn't ended due to the Great De-evolution. She passes by Leonardo, who tried to pattern his artwork after the great master, only with a *Mona Lisa* who possessed slightly less expression and a *Last Supper* with people sitting idle in their chairs instead of enjoying a meal—Block versions in place of the people the real Leonardo had once captured.

She pauses at Karen's cot.

Karen was sure, since the first signs of the Great De-evolution, that it was being caused by genetically modified crops. There was no proof that this was true—scientists never proved a link between the engineered foods and the mutated protein which caused the onset of the Great De-evolution—but Karen held firm: "Do you think you can genetically alter food and expect it to *not* impact you?" She asked this of anyone who would listen.

There were people who said God created the Great De-evolution, the same way he created everything else. Some said Satan was to blame. Some scientists put out a paper saying it must have been caused by a long dormant gene that had spread across the world over hundreds of years until it was finally triggered. They did not hazard a guess on what may have caused it to finally trigger. (This is where Karen would yell at whoever was next to her: "It was the genetically engineered foods!") Others said it might be the human body's failed way of trying to fight off environmental toxins. There was too much pollution in the air and people couldn't handle it anymore.

Through all of these possible reasons, Karen never wavered in her claims: "Do you think you can go in a lab, inject plague cells into the foods we put into our bodies, and everything will be normal? People amaze me! We aren't consumers, we're lab rats." Karen couldn't speak about the subject for more than a minute or two before getting exasperated and cussing out the entire world.

Instead of finding an excuse for why it happened, Morgan tries to relate the Great De-evolution back to the past she knows. History always repeats itself. As soon as she heard this for the first time she became a history buff. All through her life, events could be made to seem a little more bearable if she could relate them back to things that had happened in the past.

So is the Great De-evolution close to how the dinosaurs became extinct? Maybe it wasn't a meteor at all. Maybe all the dinosaurs woke up one day unable to produce baby dinosaurs that could move. She knows this isn't true, but the idea makes her feel better because it lets her believe something else will eventually evolve from man's ashes and claim the earth for itself in another million years.

What other parts of the Great De-evolution, she wonders, might have something in common with world history? Her food processor comes to mind. It was only created because calamity inspired invention. The same way the atomic bomb was created out of a necessity to end World War II, the food processor, a machine capable of keeping her well fed without farms or grocery stores, was created to end man's reliance on anyone else as everyone slowly disappeared.

The baby boom that occurred after World War II was mirrored by a comparatively small baby boom that took place when the Great De-evolution was signaled. Everyone with any inclination to have a child decided to have one as quickly as possible before the percentage of normal babies declined and the chances of having a Block became too great.

The treaties that followed the Great War's conclusion were similar to the ways various countries and continents came together to deal with the end of man. World leaders met one last time to share ideas, shake hands for photographers, and feel important. The European Union disbanded in favor of a truly borderless Europe. In America, the Survival Bill, in which a single-minded effort was put forward to create food processors, energy generators, and incinerators for every family, was passed.

She tries to think of some lesson that can be learned by history repeating itself throughout time until she is here, now, alone. But as much as she tries, she cannot see any lesson in previous species becoming extinct or the suffering that others have faced in earlier generations. She does not see how history repeating itself could have prevented the Great De-evolution or put her in a better situation in her final days. There was no lesson that would have changed the course of her life, that would have kept her from ending up as the caretaker of more people than she can look after.

There must be a lesson, she tells herself. *Maybe not to be learned from history, but there has to be a lesson somewhere. Or else, what's the point?*

She knows absolutely nothing, except for understanding that she doesn't know anything. What is the point of everything? If she just keeps trying, an answer has to be found eventually. Then everything will make sense.

24

She finds herself wondering if it's good to be hopeful for better days, for a happy ending, for something to take her away from all of this. Or is being hopeful only going to lead to disappointment? Her current predicament does not give her much to be optimistic about. Hoping for someone to come and rescue her is a waste of time; there is no one else left. Equally pointless is hoping for something, other than human extinction, to end the Great De-evolution. The days of praying for a cure are long gone. Any hope that the same process which caused the Blocks to appear in the first place will somehow reverse itself has long since passed.

She has the option to hope for a quick, painless death, but that's not something she would ever look forward to because she only knows how to survive. Her days are filled with disorder and a staggering amount of chores, with being so tired and busy that she barely has time to daydream, but nothing can change that she was raised to think each day is a treasure. Nothing that has ever happened or will ever happen can dent this lesson. Anticipation of the next day is something that should always be treasured.

She is neither an optimist nor a pessimist, but someone who simply accepts the world for what it is and gets by each day as best as she can. If she were an optimist she would not be able to kill any of the Blocks, not even for the greater good of the entire group, because a hope would linger that their circumstances might change. She would be paralyzed by the prayer that things could, somehow, get better. She would be blindly cheerful as the Blocks in her care started to die anyway because she wouldn't have enough time or energy to continue caring for all of them. That is what optimism would do. Blind hope is not everything it's cracked up to be.

But likewise, if she were a defeatist, she would have nothing to look forward to. Each day would be filled with suffering for the sake of suffering. Nothing else. She might as well kill all the Blocks in one great massacre. What would be the point to keeping them alive? So they can suffer alongside her? There would be no hope that circumstances could get any better. She might as well kill herself, too. That's what pessimism does.

No. Neither extreme will get her through this.

She is afraid of even a small dose of either outlook. If a little optimism sneaks in, how would she handle the eventual deflation when she has to send another Block to the incinerator? But on the other hand, if she notices the first traces of pessimism hovering over her, how would she ever find something positive to counterbalance the hopelessness? All she has is the group home and her wards. That is not enough to wash away dark thoughts if they began to creep in. Before long, she wouldn't care what happened to her Blocks or to herself.

That is why she remains objective and tries, sometimes without much success, to get through each day as though she is witnessing someone else's life rather than controlling her own. Almost clinically, she refuses to allow herself to be swayed toward either direction. She wakes each morning, not with hopes or fears, only determination. She goes to sleep each evening, not with prayers or begging demands, but exhaustion. There is nothing else.

There was a Canadian woman, back when Morgan

was first volunteering at the group shelter, who had stayed in contact with her brother, who has remained behind. She had come south during the first waves of migrations. He had stayed behind until everyone else was gone. Over the years, she gave up any hope of ever seeing him again, until one day he wrote and said he had found a way to travel south and would see her soon. Progress was slow, but month after month he told her of the cities he passed on the way to Miami.

The woman, filled with hope for the first time in a long time, looked younger and happier than Morgan had ever seen her. And then, her brother, somewhere between Maryland and North Carolina, stopped sending updates. She never heard from him again. She never found out what happened to him, and the joy she had experienced with the anticipation of seeing him again turned to anguish at not knowing how he died. Was it a heart attack? Did animals kill him? Had he fallen through a weakened bridge, or had he simply given up the quest in an area without internet access? She drove herself crazy thinking of all the ways her brother might have died. The once rejuvenated women suddenly looked not only as old as she had prior to the excitement, but many years older. After allowing herself that hope and then having it taken away, she gave up on everything. She died a month later.

That woman's fate is why Morgan doesn't want anything to look forward to and also why she doesn't allow herself any pity. Just to make sure Daniel never replied, she still checks her e-mail occasionally. But even this is done with a cold indifference; she doesn't expect to find a response and thus doesn't feel let down when there are no new messages.

The Blocks encompass the two extremes of being hopeful and being melancholy on her behalf. In the middle of quadrant 2 is her pair of pilots. Although not from the same parents, the two men could be mistaken as twins. Both Blocks have bushy eyebrows, hazel eyes, and pointed chins. Both have sagging earlobes and small nostrils. She can only tell them apart because Richard has a slight dent between his eyebrows that makes him look like he is constantly frowning, while Roger does not.

She marvels at how two different sets of parents in different places of the country could have children that ended up looking so alike. And not only that, but that the two families ended up in the same final community and the same Block group home within that final community. The coincidence is a daily reminder of how amazing the world can be sometimes.

Looking at the two pilots, she wonders what it must have been like to fly a plane or helicopter and survey the earth as the population declined. The couple of times Morgan flew on planes when she was younger, she remembered being eager to look out the window during takeoff and landing to see what the city, the farm land, the roads, all of it, looked like from the sky. How different the experience must be without people bustling about everywhere. Her two pilots have vastly different outlooks on what they saw as they flew over the land.

Roger and Richard were the last pilots healthy enough to fly helicopters. They knew how to fly planes, too, but runways deteriorated, preventing successful takeoffs and landings. With their helicopters, though, these two pilots would get to see a landscape that once held so much life but now resembled an artist's rendition of life. Each town they saw would be more of a model of what a town once was than a real place where people lived.

They would take off at the same time. Both pilots would see the highways are still there. However, now all eight lanes of these super-sized roads are empty, except for where cars were abandoned in the places they broke down. The shopping centers are empty. So are the fairgrounds. The churches are still there, but now only for show. Giant sports stadiums sit unoccupied. They look just like the real thing, albeit rusted and faded, but no fans cheer on their teams. This replica of a real world would either be fascinating or upsetting.

Roger would see a landscape void of cars inching along in rush-hour traffic. No longer are all eight lanes filled with thousands of steady streams of exhaust coming from tailpipes. A series of golf courses and parks have been given back to the animals. A segmented land, divided into municipalities and counties by various roads and highways, is slowly being covered in a blanket of green that makes everything look like it's less a land of boundaries and more a single continuation of the places we once knew.

He would survey the empty parking lots, the abandoned office buildings, and when he landed he would tell everyone how amazing it was to see the world in this fashion. It was like seeing a hint of what the world must have looked like before man put metal and plastic everywhere.

"You have to see this," he would say to everyone upon landing. "It's still the world we knew, but without horns honking, people stuck at red lights, or sirens flashing. It's beautiful."

Richard wouldn't have the same outlook. After taking off, he would see the abandoned cars on the side of the highways. He wouldn't be able to help but wonder what happened to each family. Did they get to where they wanted to go, or did they get stranded on the way there? What was each person doing in the moments leading up to the flat tire or broken axle that left them stranded away from home? He would see empty theme parks and remember how his favorite memories from childhood were spent on the loud, fast rides. He doesn't have any children of his own to take to the park. No one does. He would also see a zoo still overflowing with animals, but without anyone to clean up after them or keep them sequestered in their own areas. Zebras and giraffes would quickly be wiped out. Almost all of the cute animals would be eaten. A couple of leopards and tigers would still roam the land, but even these were never well suited to the concrete prison built around them.

This pilot would see cemeteries covered with weeds,

the dead forgotten behind a veil of green. There would be a giant hill next to a cemetery, perfectly round in shape. Was it one of the rumored Block mass-graves? Nearby, the roof of a library has collapsed, thousands of books ruined over the course of months. Death, disorder, deterioration—everywhere.

Richard wouldn't land his helicopter to tell anyone else what he saw. What would he say that could prepare someone for the loss of everything they once knew? It wouldn't suffice to say, "I hope you're ready for what you'll see once you're up there." Nor would, "It's not going to be anything like the world you once loved," be able to brace them for it.

He wouldn't be able to stand the sights, wouldn't think anyone else should have to see them either. His helicopter would take a nose-dive into the nearest lake. If there were still people nearby, they might find bits and pieces of the exploded craft floating on the water's surface. But most of it, the pilot included, would sink to the bottom, vanishing like the rest of his world.

Elaine would have wanted to be Roger more than Richard. Who wouldn't? At least she would be happy when she died. Who would want to be Richard and be miserable every day?

She reaches over, disconnects Richard's feeding tube from its nutrient bag, then begins to walk away. She pauses, though, turns back around, and disconnects Roger's tube as well. They are twins in almost everything, she reasons, it wouldn't be fair to take one now and not the other. And, she knows, taking one body away has not done anything to help keep her on schedule with her chores.

Maybe tomorrow, with two fewer people to care for, she will finally get done with her rounds before midnight.

The thought sounds suspiciously like a hope.

25

Another storm. There is no rain this time, though, only wind. It's the type of storm that idiot weathermen used to stand outside in to demonstrate to their viewers just how strong the winds were. She hears howls as if a great pack of coyotes has congregated in Miami and is looking for any last remnants of mankind to eat. There are screams and shrieks, and they affect her concentration as she moves from cot to cot. She imagines boats being thrown around the city, homes being torn to pieces and tossed down the street. After consideration, she realizes she has no way of knowing if there are any boats left to throw around. They may all have been sunk already in the previous years. Without repairs after each storm, there may not be any houses standing either. There may not even be a city. She could walk outside, look toward the skyline, and gasp at the sight: a wasteland where towers of brilliant steel once cast shadows over the entire area.

"I'd hate to be out in this weather," she tells Ruiz, the Block she happens to be caring for in quadrant 1 as a sheet of metal whines overhead. Instead of focusing on the roof, something she cannot control, she tells Ruiz this is the exact kind of storm that her grandparents' house was destroyed in.

"That was back when I was eight," she says. "Or nine. I don't know. It was such a long time ago it seems like someone else's life."

"I found a kidnapped girl one time in the middle of a storm like this," he says. "Some guy was trying to sneak away with her, telling people she was his Block daughter. Happened all the time during the migrations, when everyone was making their way south."

Ruiz always wanted to be important. It wasn't until the Great De-evolution had been playing out for a decade that he realized his calling in life in the form of a young woman wandering the highway. He found her between Dayton and Columbus. The woman's family thought she was either dead or had run away to one of the southern settlements. When Ruiz saw her walking down the highway, he knew something wasn't right. She didn't know where she was, didn't remember who she was, didn't have any identification. Ruiz took her to the closest police station, where they were able to identify her before sending her to the hospital for medical treatment. She had simply gotten sick, the nature of her sickness being one that ravaged her mind. On her own, wandering the streets, it didn't take long before she looked like she was a drug-addicted loner. A hundred other people had seen her walking down the highway that day, but no one had stopped except for Ruiz.

The experience changed his life. Without a family of his own, without a job that society needed anymore, he set about traveling all across the country trying to reconnect missing people with their families. Sometimes he had to deliver bad news—a body found in a trash dump, the remains of a missing person found in a burned out car—but there were also times that made it all worth it: a report that a long lost brother was living happily in San Diego, the knowledge that a daughter had moved to Houston where she was married and working in a food processor factory.

It was only because of the Great De-evolution and the abundance of missing people that resulted from it that Ruiz found a way to feel important, found a way to live a life that he considered worthwhile.

Maybe life is about how long it takes you to find your true calling, and all the good you can do after you discover it.

"It's perfect weather for covering up a murder," he tells Morgan. "Or for disappearing yourself and having everyone think you were a victim of the storm."

A loud scream of wind rattles the group home as if agreeing with him.

"Why would anyone want to do something like that?" Morgan asks.

"You'd be surprised."

This is how Ruiz speaks, as if his time looking for people has taught him valuable lessons about human nature, lessons that might be better off if they were kept private.

"Well, I'd certainly never try to do something foolish like that," she tells him.

"And I thank you for that."

"Why would you thank me?"

"Because if you're trying to sneak out in the middle of the storm," he tells her in his sober monotone, "it means the rest of us here are pretty much fucked."

"Of course," she says, thinks about saying something else, but a terrible shriek of wind shakes the metal, tempts it to rip away.

It takes a full minute for the gust to pass. She watches the roof the entire time, suspecting that this will be the storm that is finally victorious. But after the wind has gone, the roof is still intact. She has forgotten what else she was going to say.

"It's okay," Ruiz says. "Just yell if you think of it later. I'll still be here."

"Thanks, Ruiz. I will."

She moves to the next bed. There are forty more men and women who need to be cleaned and repositioned. She cannot spend too much time talking to each one or else she will fall behind schedule again.

26

In her care, she has a Christian, a Jew, a Muslim, and a Hindu. They are all in the same row in quadrant 2. Elaine had groaned at their inclusion in the game of assigning identities to each Block, saying they were supposed to be surrounded by celebrities and by people who never got a fair shot at a normal life, not by people that would just as soon judge you for your beliefs and look down on you if you didn't believe the same things they did.

"It's not like that," Morgan had protested.

Elaine's passive-aggressive response to Morgan's four religious Blocks was the creation of an atheist Block. She resides in the next row over from the ones Morgan created—Elaine's payback for tainting her game.

Elaine had offered a devilish smile before saying, on behalf of her Block, "She refuses to believe in God just because it irritates the people in the row in front of her."

"Don't be like that," Morgan had said. "I'm just trying to get as wide a variety of people as possible."

Elaine shot back, "How do you know the detective, the painter, or the singer aren't religious? Their religion doesn't define them."

"But neither does their occupation."

Elaine rolled her eyes and said, "Oh my god, you are

so awful at this game."

That had been the end of the conversation. And while Elaine was always eager to hear more details about the comedian, the mad scientist, and the world traveler, she never asked for more tidbits on those four religious Blocks.

What Elaine had failed to understand was that Morgan's four religious Blocks didn't care what anyone else believed. None of them had ever tried to push their views on the others around them, and none of them ever would. They got along with each other as though there was no real difference at all. None of them think to themselves that they belong to the correct religion, and none of them pity the rest for not being so fortunate. None of them think they are going to heaven while the others will be excluded just because they belong to a different religion. She admires them for being adamant in their beliefs while being accepting of other faiths. That is why she had wanted them included in the Block game even though Elaine had protested.

She has no core beliefs of her own, doesn't, really, believe in anything. Maybe that is another reason she wanted to be amongst them. In the back of her mind she can't help but think it's odd that she has created a Christian who was raised by Christian parents, a Muslim who was raised by Muslim parents, and so on, yet her own parents were very religious and she never grew up believing the same things they believed in. If there is a difference between them, between the believers who learned from their parents and herself, who was unable to believe what she was told, she is unable to identify it. Maybe they were better students. Maybe her parents weren't persuasive enough. Does the reason make any difference?

She wonders if her Blocks realize how different their beliefs might be if they had been born to another set of parents who belonged to a different religion. Do they realize they wouldn't be any more right or wrong if they grew up believing in something else? Or do they simply rationalize that their God's plan started for them by putting them in the wombs of mothers who lived in a country where the correct religion was practiced?

She has never been able to ask her religious Blocks this question for fear that each of them would tell her she is a murderer in the eyes of God.

But how can they believe so staunchly in the things they have been told if they only believe them because they were taught to? Is that what faith is? There is nothing in her life that she trusts just because she has been told that she should trust it. She hadn't even believed it when, in elementary school, her science teacher said a feather and a rock fall at the same speed. She had raised her hand and demanded that he either stop joking around or perform the experiment in front of the class. Of course, the feather and rock had landed on the ground at the same time.

Maybe she would be better off after all if she could have faith in something the way they do.

Only her Buddhist Block has come to terms with his religion on his own. As a child, her Buddhist was taught to believe in one thing, but as he grew up he thought about why that religion had been created in the first place, thought of all the people that had been kept down by its beliefs, and how the teachings had changed over the years to try and explain science's latest discoveries. The other Blocks snicker at the Buddhist for believing that you can be reborn in another life, without realizing the idea of reincarnation was in the Bible for hundreds of years before it was removed. It turns out that allowing people to think they could be reincarnated, allowing them to make up for their sins in future lives, made it unnecessarily difficult to control them in their current life. So, Morgan wonders, were the original Christians wrong to believe in reincarnation, or are current Christians wrong to mock it? And who had the authority to remove that idea from the Bible if the Bible was God's word? This is exactly why she's glad she doesn't have anything to believe in.

There are days in which she tries to decide if it is better to believe something just because it offers comfort, or if it's better to go through her days just trying to get by as best as she can. Will she get to the end of her life and realize she was wrong the entire time? Will she get to the gates of heaven and realize she won't be allowed entrance because she was a skeptic?

Afterlife? Ha! It's rapidly approaching and yet she still doesn't know whether to be afraid or to look forward to it. Both of her parents died knowing exactly what they believed—that they would go to heaven and be reunited with loved ones. This knowledge comforted them. Why can't Morgan believe the same thing? What is it that makes her doubt that possibility when the Blocks in front of her have always accepted what their parents taught them?

Is it too much to ask for some little bit of proof? If she could just be given a glimpse of heaven or of the existence of God she would be a staunch believer, too. Does needing some bit of proof make her a heathen? Does it mean she is going to hell? She doesn't even believe in hell. Does that mean she will have one of the best seats in the fiery house?

If asking for a sign is asking for too much, how else are you supposed to truly believe on your own? The only other way is to believe what you are told, and that hasn't worked for her. Even when there were others around, each trying to convince her that their beliefs were the ones that would earn her salvation, none of it sounded convincing.

How is one book of beliefs better than another? They were all written by men and taught by men. Doesn't that make them all the same? Throughout history, they have each gone to war with the others simply because men of faith told them to. Doesn't that make them all questionable?

Elaine's atheist is no better. Elaine made a point by saying the non-believer just wants to be different, just wants to piss people off. Not believing in something just because you are stubborn is just as bad as believing in something for no better reason than you are told to believe it. There has to be a middle ground. There has to be something she can find that makes sense for her. Her Blocks won't help her find it, though.

She thinks Elaine's atheist would have been more convincing if she had turned away from religion because of all the pain and hurt and suffering she saw everywhere. The atheist might have swayed Morgan if she hadn't been so smug. If she had offered a pained smile and, while looking at the Blocks littered everywhere throughout the gymnasium, said, "Why would I waste any time thinking about God if this is what He does to us?" then that would have been something Morgan could consider.

How could God be good if he allowed millions to die of starvation and genocide in Africa, allowed war to ravage the earth, without interruption, for hundreds of years, and created diseases that would destroy good-hearted people while avoiding the wicked? These are the things Elaine could have said on behalf of her Atheist Block if she hadn't been so busy trying to prove a point. Everything this Block saw was a reason not to believe in God: a family traveling south that got stuck on the side of the road; a man trying to take care of his brother, only to be eaten by wolves; a woman trying to get her family back to her homeland, drowning in the middle of the ocean after a small leak turned into a big leak.

If she assigned herself a story, what would it be? Would it be that she became disillusioned by the stupid things her clergymen said, as if the Bible should be taken literally? Would she see herself as the girl in high school who had gone out on a date with a Jewish boy only to find out his parents wouldn't allow their son to marry outside their religion? Uh, marry? She had only been a freshman in high school—that one date hardly called for a marriage announcement. But at least she knew how they had felt about her. Would she see herself as the roommate of a Muslim girl who was extremely happy, but only after getting away from the horrific men who thought girls shouldn't be allowed to go to school? Or is her story that she found Buddhism shortly after college and liked it, but didn't like any wisdom that taught you to be walked over?

She wants to believe in something, she just isn't sure what.

Aristotle, her world traveler, seems to feed off her doubt: "I've seen the entire world, and yet I feel like I still have so much more to learn."

"All of those places you saw are quiet now," she says, remembering the Grand Canyon and how calm it had been even when there were other people around. "I don't know if there is time left to learn anything else. But you will always have the memories."

She reaches down and disconnects his nutrient bag from the line running into his forearm.

"You will always have the memories," she says again.

And for one last night Aristotle will go to sleep believing whatever it is he has grown to understand about the world during all his travels, about people and their purpose on this planet, about what else is out there and what can never be known.

She finishes her rounds, exhausted like always, and goes to sleep before she can ask any more questions.

She thinks of the Grand Canyon's majestic, rugged landscape again the next morning when she uses the forklift to carry Aristotle's body to the flames. Whatever he learned goes into the fire with him.

27

She knows something is wrong as soon as she opens her eyes and looks to her bedside table to see what time it is.

The clock isn't there.

It's always there. She is the only one who could have moved it. Thinking she might have brushed it to the floor in her sleep, her eyes scan the ground next to her bed. Nothing there either. It has simply vanished.

That's when she notices something else that isn't right: the lights are on throughout the group home. She always turns the lights off before going to bed. Ever since she was a young girl, she couldn't sleep in a room where there were lights on, no matter how tired she was. It is even more impossible for her to sleep with the gym's over-sized industrial bulbs glaring down on her. Not to mention how uncomfortable she is when she can see the faces of all the bodies littered across the floor.

Her breathing stops. Leonardo, one of her painters, is looking at her from across the room. She tries to take another breath but her lungs are clenched.

It's only a dream, she tells herself. The thought does nothing to help calm her fright, however.

Her hands are balled fists. Even though the blanket is over her, she feels completely exposed. There is no mistaking that Leonardo is looking at her and not simply staring in her general direction. His head could have fallen to one side, but that doesn't explain the way his eyes focus on her. They leave her just long enough to scan the entire room, then return to her. His eyes are calculating.

She knows exactly what he is doing. He is making sure no one is around to stop him from coming across the room so he can wrap his hands around her little throat. He is making sure a security camera isn't recording this, verifying no other Blocks are awake to question what is going on. From the way his eyes scan for witnesses, she knows he means to hurt her and hurt her badly.

Maybe he will crush her windpipe and get it over with quickly. She can only pray that whatever he does to her is not drawn out. She doesn't want to suffer. But, she fears, he might strangle her just hard enough that her throat burns and her vision starts to black out, only to release his grip until she regains her senses, then starting the process all over again. Maybe he will choke her, let her recover, choke her, let her recover, for an entire night, until she is begging him just to let her die. She imagines the way he laughs each time she begins a new round of gagging, the way his chin raises in victory, proud, each time he allows her to gasp for air.

Or maybe he will clench his hands into fists, the way hers currently are, and use them against her. She can do nothing with her hands—she is paralyzed again—but there is an endless list of things he can do to her. He won't hit her too hard at first. However, as she begs to be left alone, he will begin to strike her with more force. After a while, both of her eyes will be swollen shut. She will no longer be able to see when each strike is about to land, will no longer be able to clench her jaw against the pounding. This won't keep him from continuing the onslaught. He will keep hitting her until the majority of her teeth are knocked out. Some will bounce off the hard floor. Others will fall back in her throat, resting against her tonsils. Eventually, her jaw will break. She will look like a monster.

Without a working mouth, there is no way she can beg to be left alone. Hard fragments of broken teeth will cut her lips. She will want to plead with him to stop beating her, but he will only look down with scorn and ask if Cindy or Aristotle or Roger deserved to starve to death. Without giving her a chance to answer, he will begin raining more strikes down.

From across the room she can see all of this in his eyes.

Thank God he can't get up and come over here since he's—NO! Oh my god, no!

Right as she watches, her hands still clenching her blanket as if it offers protection, she sees, with her very own eyes, that Leonardo can move.

Slowly, one arm changes from being perfectly straight, the hand halfway between his hip and knee, to bending until it is at his waist. The hand, one of the hands that will torture her, braces against the edge of the cot.

He's coming for me! He's going to kill me.

The painter steadies himself against the side of his cot, his hand pulling himself upright. His other elbow pushes against the mattress. His eyes never part from hers. They do not even blink. Nor does he smile to let her know this is a joke. He simply looks at her as if she is already dead.

The look in those eyes makes her want to scream, but she cannot. They make her want to flee the gymnasium, go running into the street, but she cannot do that either. There is nothing she can do. Nothing at all except wait for him to move closer and begin hitting her.

Sitting upright, Leonardo pauses to inspect his surroundings, his eyes reminding her that she is nothing.

Maybe he's looking for something to hit me with.

He will have no problem finding a tool that can do as much damage as his hands. A pair of old pliers are on the ground next to a box of supplies. He can place these on her nose and slowly increase the pressure until the cartilage crumbles away. Or maybe he is looking for gloves so her blood doesn't get all over him, so that when he covers her nose with one hand and her mouth with the other, none of her snot gets on him.

Please, God, no. Please, no!

Her eyes burst open. The alarm clock is next to her. The gym's lights are off. Leonardo is lying on his cot like all the other Blocks.

She is drenched with sweat. Her clothes are soaked. Looking down, she realizes she is still gripping the blanket with her balled hands, the same way she was in her dream. One hand releases its grip and feels her face. No bruises. No bleeding. Nothing broken. She sighs and puts her head back on the pillow. There will be no more sleep for the night. Not after that.

She has begun to realize that what happens to her in her dreams is happening when she wakes up. If she is struggling to breathe in her nightmare, she wakes to discover she has been holding her breath. If she is gripping the blanket in her sleep, her hands are in the same position when she opens her eyes. The same thing goes for her sweating, her crying, all of it.

This realization leads to a second thought: if what she is doing in her dreams actually happens in real life, what will happen when one of these Blocks makes good on their promise to kill her? If she is being strangled in her nightmare, will she stop breathing in real life? If she is poisoned in her dream, will her very real, very critical body organs begin to shut down? Will she awake to find her eyeballs have been ripped from her face or her tongue lying on the pillow next to her bloody mouth? Will she awake at all? A feeling in the back of her head, one she can't shake, says the moment one of her Blocks kills her in her nightmare, she will die in real life.

"What do you want from me?" she yells to the entire room. The only response is the sound of her voice echoing back at her, asking her the same question. "I'm trying my best. What more can I do? I'm trying my best."

She begins crying then. Not because of the dream she just had, but because she knows this plea to everyone and everything that can hear her won't be enough to keep her from having a similar nightmare the next night.

28

Her job is made somewhat easier by her wards' inability to complain. In her care, she has people from every walk of life, possessing every possible political ideology, coming from every ethnicity, and yet there has never been even a hint of an argument between them.

It was obvious that if a new generation couldn't speak or move, they wouldn't be able to bear arms. The appearance of the Blocks marked the first time in over three centuries that humans didn't try to kill each other over some kind of trivial argument. No war between countries, no war between a country and its rebels, not even fighting between two warring tribes. It took the emergence of humans that couldn't do anything for themselves for everyone else in the world to stop killing each other. Anything else—rampant disease, enlightenment toward a higher consciousness—had failed to be enough for people to stop blowing each other up.

It was for this reason that the final Nobel Peace prize ever awarded was given to the Blocks. Not to a specific Block in a specific country, but to the entire generation of people that didn't become indoctrinated to hate those of other colors, from other countries, or holding different beliefs.

There was nothing intentional about the peace they created, however, and this caused everyone else to resent the world's most prestigious award being given to the very people that were causing mankind's extinction. It wasn't as though the Blocks were leading a peaceful resistance by marching through the streets or having a sit-in until their pleas were heard. They weren't going on hunger strikes or declaring themselves conscientious objectors. If they were, the award would have had some merit behind it. The Blocks weren't refusing to continue fighting in wars, they were simply incapable of doing anything.

Although it received more hate mail than it had ever received before, the Nobel committee stood behind its decision. It was, though, the last year they gave the award. They said this was because the Blocks brought about true and everlasting peace, that no more awards were necessary because there was no more injustice to stand against. The Blocks had done that.

Her literary Block in row 3 of quadrant 1 grumbles at the thought of the Nobel committee ending its awards. Irving swears that if it hadn't been for the Great De-evolution, he would have eventually won the Nobel Prize for literature. Even with the Great De-evolution in full swing, he managed to write the Great American Novel and became regarded as the final generation's version of Hemingway and Steinbeck. Had the publishers still been around, his books would have been translated into every imaginable language, would have made girls in Malaysia weep, made farmers in the Ukraine compassionate, made monks in Argentina laugh.

All of Irving's stories revolved around the end of the world.

"Yeah? Like what?" Elaine had asked the first time she heard of this Block's achievements, causing Morgan to scramble for the details.

At thirty, Irving broke onto the literary scene with a romantic story of star-crossed Block lovers, who, although their families were no longer around to care one way or the other about a budding romance, were still separated: the lovers came from rival group homes. The caretakers from one home despised the caretakers from the opposing home and vice versa. For years, the pair of enemy houses had minor quarrels. They didn't even allow the Blocks from one home to be near the Blocks from the other home.

But two caretakers, one from either house, set about ending the feud. To do this, one of them brought a young woman from her group home and the other brought a young man from his group home and they had the two Blocks attend a dance together. This didn't bring about an end to the feud, however. It escalated it. To stop the fighting that ensued, the pair of caretakers decided to give their respective Blocks a fake poison in order to make the other house think the Block was dead. But, alas, a different caretaker, one who didn't realize the Block was still alive, had the young lover put into an incinerator. If PEN awards were still being given, this would have received one.

Later in his career, Irving wrote of a king with three Block daughters for whom he divides his kingdom. The Block daughters don't try to outwit each other or the king, but their caretakers do. With one of the Block daughters and her caretaker banished, the king begins to go insane. By the end, all three of his Block daughters have been murdered and the king dies full of despair. If Pulitzers were still being awarded, this would have been the unanimous winner.

At the peak of his career, Irving wrote a novel about a group home for Blocks in which one of the caretakers tries to be the dictator of all the others. Most of the other workers celebrate having someone so passionate about their cause, but three of them conspire to assassinate the ambitious man. After his death, another group of three forms, but this one seeks revenge for the caretaker's murder. Amongst rows of Blocks, each lying peacefully in their cots, the two triumvirates of caretakers quarrel until one of them, guilt-ridden, commits suicide. The novel ends with the last remaining caretaker declaring how noble his fellow caretakers were. The only people to hear this speech are the hundreds of bodies that require nutrient bags in order to stay alive. And this is where, if they were still awarding Nobel Prizes for literature, Irving would have received one.

And yet no one has read Irving's novels. Nor will they ever read them. His audience is dead. What remains is a group of impostors that resemble an audience. So very unfair.

It is already noon and Morgan has barely made any progress in the day's chores. She reaches over and disconnects Irving's nutrient bag from the line running into his forearm. Without waiting her feet shuffle across the concrete to where the next Block waits for her care.

"I'm sorry," she says, looking back at her writer.

Irving does not reply.

29

Each day she has one fewer Block to care for, but each day her body endures another round of abuse. There is no way a woman of her age should be on her feet all day. And not just on her feet, but walking from bed to bed, shoving with all her weight behind her just to get each body into a new position. It does not matter if one less Block means she is able to finish by midnight; the amount of work she does each day is just too much. Even if she could somehow get to bed by eight o'clock or even nine o'clock, it wouldn't matter. Her body is too old for this fight day after day without a break.

Old women aren't meant to get up before the sun, work all through the day and night, and then do the same thing again for weeks at a time. It is a feat that people thirty years younger shouldn't be trying. Over ninety years old, her body has no hope of standing up to the fatigue. It's not long before she is sick.

Her body simply shuts down. The morning after Irving is sent to the incinerator, she opens her eyes, but that is all she can do. Her first thought is that this must be another nightmare if she is helpless in bed, but it is sunny outside and birds are chirping. These are things that don't happen in her nightmares. And she is able to groan, yet another sign she isn't about to be tormented by one of her Blocks.

Her body, still on her cot, is wracked with shaking and trembling that is beyond her control. Her arms bounce off her ribs without her being able to still them. Her teeth clatter. She alternates between shivering, even when under three blankets, and feeling like she must be directly under the notorious Miami sun. Her clothes are soaked so that, by the time the shivering starts again, she is even colder than before.

Thoughts enter her mind—*I have to start my rounds*—but just as quickly her eyes flutter momentarily before closing again. The next time they open, half the day has passed. She is feeling no better. It takes all of her strength to reach for the glass of water on her bedside table. She gulps it down without any care that it's the only water within reach.

The next time she awakens, she reaches for the same glass of water. Only when it's in her grasp does she remember drinking it hours earlier. Even the small movement of sitting up to drink leaves her head spinning.

An odor hits her. Urine. As bad as her sense of smell is, the piss must be her own if she can smell it. She is lying in her own mess. Too weak and unbalanced to move, there is nothing she can do but close her eyes and go back to sleep once more.

It is the middle of the night when she opens her eyes again. Her stomach is grumbling. Hunger adds to her weakness. Her mouth is dry. There is nothing to eat or drink within reach. The area she uses as a makeshift kitchen is twenty feet away. Just looking in that direction makes her head feel like it will wobble right off her neck and fall on the floor. The room appears to tumble in circles. There is no way she can make it the short distance to the kitchen. With her head still spinning, with no strength, she would end up in the middle of the floor, unable to move back to her bed or inch closer toward the food and water.

If she doesn't get nourishment soon, though, she will die right in her bed. And, with her, the remaining fifty Blocks. The world will end with one person failing the very people she is meant to care for. It is not an end she will accept.

The only other thing near her is a half-empty box of nutrient bags for her Blocks. She reaches toward them, her eyes closed because that makes the spinning less severe, and withdraws one nutrient bag and one IV. It takes all of her concentration just to uncap the tip of the nutrient bag and then spin its connector onto its feed line.

She moans with exhaustion.

Once the nutrient bag is ready, she uncaps the other end of the tube. A needle is exposed. Without much care, certainly without the care she gives her Blocks when she is healthy, she jabs the needle into her forearm.

The last thought that goes through her head is, *That didn't hurt at all; just a little prick really.*

And then she passes out again.

30

A second day passes in the same haze of sickness and fatigue. On the third day, she is finally able to lift herself out of bed. As soon as she moves, though, she wishes she were back asleep. Her clothes, the sheets, and the mattress all smell like garbage. The smell of urine and shit that she has been able to avoid due to her aging senses finally fills her nose, but instead of being caused by her Blocks is produced by her. There is no way to know how many times she dirtied the mattress while she was asleep.

How ironic that I spend my days changing everyone around me, and now no one is around to help me when I'm filthy.

She remains there, on her back, thinking. The less she moves while she formulates a game plan, the less of a mess there will be to clean up. There is no point to getting out of bed right away just to distance herself from the filth. She has been lying in it for two days; what is another couple of minutes? There is no shame, nothing to be embarrassed about. No one is around to see her predicament or to judge her for remaining in her own excrement.

It's important to make sure her equilibrium is back. If she were to dart out of bed too quickly, she might become lightheaded and fall flat on the concrete. She props herself up on one arm. The room is not spinning in circles; her vision seems steady.

She looks around the gutted gymnasium, tries to think of the best course of action for her Blocks. The nutrient bags all have the same regulator, meaning they will all provide each Block with the same steady amount of nutrition day and night. Looking down at her own bag, she sees it is nearly empty, meaning that in the two days that have passed, the Blocks have only been without food and water for maybe eight hours. Twelve hours max.

The priorities she comes up with, in order, are: get food and water for herself so she can regain her strength and function properly, determine the living from the dead, refill the nutrient bags of the living, get herself cleaned off. After all of that is done, she can worry about getting the dead Blocks to the incinerator. The luxury of not having the living in beds next to the dead will have to be put on hold for a while.

If she tries to do any more than this, if she tries to work around the clock until everyone is cared for again, she will relapse into a bedridden mess. Her body is weaker than it has ever been. She is used to hobbling to get from one place to another. She is even used to arthritic fingers and not being able to taste much of the food she eats unless she adds a spoon full of salt to it. But she is not used to feeling utterly and completely feeble in her old age. This is how people die without realizing they have deteriorated away to nothing. Her dry mouth, her dirty clothes, the nutrient bag still connected to her arm, all remind her she is no longer the young person she used to be.

Maybe life starts the first time you understand your own limitations and is measured by the ways you exceed those boundaries.

The stench of shit reminds her that she needs to start moving.

The living Blocks, however many are left, won't be repositioned and cleaned until the following day, maybe not for two more days. It depends on how much she can manage before she needs rest. It also depends on how many of her Blocks are dead and how long it takes her to transport each one to the incinerator. By the time she gets to caring for the living again, four days could easily pass. She has no idea how long it takes for bedsores to develop or for maggots to harvest from within shit-filled diapers. Hopefully, it is longer than four days.

She fills a glass with water, drinks it, refills it, and drinks that too. From the food processor, a bowl of soup is generated. It does not have much taste.

How did Daniel deal with his frailty and with the overwhelming responsibility he surely faced? Did he accept his fate, his age, his weakening body? Did he resign himself to defeat? Or did he fight the way Morgan fought until she got sick? Is his body lying on the floor in the Los Angeles group home, where he finally crumpled in exhaustion, never to get back up? Toward the end, was Daniel forced to sacrifice a couple of his Blocks for the well-being of the majority, or was his un-doing that he tried to force everyone to keep living until there was too much sickness and suffering to recover from?

Are the things that are happening to her the same things that happened in Los Angeles, Houston, and New Orleans? Did the group home in Los Angeles finally go quiet when Daniel worked himself to death? Did the final group home in Houston incur a mass starvation after the final caretaker there went to sleep one night and never woke up again? Did the caretaker at the New Orleans group home fear this possibility so much that she took matters into her own hands by burning the entire home to the ground before taking her own life?

She pushes these thoughts from her head. They are not helpful. After getting food and water for herself, she walks through the four quadrants. It's worse than she feared.

There are dead bodies everywhere. Some died with their eyes and mouths open, giving them the appearance of being frightened as life left them. These are the bodies she finds herself looking away from. Others died with their eyes closed, as if they were aware of what was happening and had resigned themselves to not being saved. To these, she apologizes.

A surprising amount of the dead are already grey, a series of grotesque sculptures aligned in rows. A few of the bodies, still with rosy flesh, trick her into thinking they are still alive. It's only when she feels for a pulse and meets the resistance of rigor mortis that she knows there will be no heartbeat. These are the bodies that make her shudder. She is used to touching these people, but touching a wrist or fingers that are locked in the freeze of death always makes her yank her hand back. It's not something she is proud of. On the contrary, she apologizes each time it happens.

The pungency of shit and death and sickness are everywhere. So pervasive is the stench of human excrement that she cannot tell which Blocks need to be changed and which merely released whatever waste they had when they died.

She can use the forklift to transport dead bodies to the incinerator, but removing a corpse does not erase the smell of death. If only the food processor could make something resembling air fresheners. For the first time in a long time she is thankful for still having good eyesight while the rest of her senses faded away.

For the Blocks that still seem healthy, she refills their bags and tells them she will be back soon to finish caring for them. For the ones that are already dead, she marks an X on one of their hands and continues on to the next bed.

Only sixteen of the fifty Blocks are still alive. Three of these appear so weak that bringing them back to health might be more torture than simply letting them die.

With her headcount done, with the nutrient bags of the living refilled, she powers up the forklift. One by one, the dead are transported to the flames, bed and all. The work takes longer than she thinks it should. Only half of the dead are gone, into the incinerator, by the time midnight comes around.

The last thing to go in the incinerator that night is her own bed. It would take more energy to change the mattress and sheets than it would to simply burn the entire cot. She can put a blanket down on one of the spare beds and sleep there. The days of being picky are gone.

The last thing she says before going to sleep is, "I'm sorry." She says this to those still living. And then, "I wish I could do more, but for one night you'll have to be stuck around the less fortunate."

For once, her Blocks are not talkative. Not a single one of them offers a reply.

The next day she transports the rest of the dead to the incinerator. With only a couple of hours left in the day, she begins cleaning and repositioning the few Blocks who have survived with her. And when she grows weak and needs a break from repositioning bodies, she sits and enjoys some food and water.

Everywhere she looks, there are pitiful reminders of what used to be an organized group home. Quadrant 4 is no longer four neatly aligned rows with four Blocks in each row. There are no more rows in quadrant 4 at all, only three bodies scattered like a misaligned constellation. Quadrant 3 only has five Blocks.

She considers reorganizing the remaining beds into neat lines, one final quadrant of survivors. It would offer a semblance of the life she once knew, maybe even fool her into being able to believe that life can continue as it had before she fell ill. But she knows this act would only be for aesthetics, would be wasted time and needless energy. And so, because of this, there are large patches of bare concrete between each body. Instead of looking like they are part of a group, each Block looks like it is slowly floating out in space, carried in random directions by other stars, by black holes, by whatever invisible forces control everything that is happening all around them.

31

A storm approaches. Its wind sounds like a plane's engine, like a great jumbo jet must be parked right outside the group home. But instead of taking her to safety, the booming noise ensures she is trapped.

The roof whines against the wind's force. The sheets overlap so that if one goes most will go. The design is intended to prevent minor leaks and to ensure the roof lasts as long as possible. Unless, of course, an entire panel is torn away. If that happens, most of the roof would fly apart and so much water will be channeled into the room that she will have to flee with whatever supplies and Blocks she can transport. She either won't get wet, or a flood will wash them away. There is no in-between.

It rains for two days straight. It thunders too, but this she barely acknowledges compared to the downpour of water and the force of the wind. She fears looking out the windows. If the streets are flooded, if the weeds are drowned under a newly formed lake, it's a matter of time until water starts rushing in. If water doesn't start coming down through the roof, it will surely come in under the doors. She will have to decide if she sticks it out with her Blocks, knowing full well that none of them will survive the sickness and mold that will get them, or if she will pack what little she still calls her own and head for the nearest suitable place to live by herself.

If it weren't for the power generator, ensuring she doesn't have to try caring for the remaining Blocks without any lights or air conditioning, they would be lost already. She would be bumping into cots until her shins were purple and she was limping everywhere she went (more than she limps already). Without music echoing through the giant room, she would be forced to hear her own feet shuffling across the floor, would have to acknowledge how loud her breathing is just from performing simple chores all day.

For two days and two nights, the rain and wind sound like they will surely wash the gym away.

This is it, she thinks, preparing herself for the end.

A splattering of water showers down on random parts of the gymnasium floor where the metal sheets are briefly lifted by the wind. The gust subsides, though, and the roof settles again. The structure remains firm.

Eventually, the rain recedes. Only after she looks up and sees sun pouring through the clouds does she allow herself to look outside at her surroundings. Further down the road, the streets are flooded. A cat, separated by an impromptu body of water from the kittens it has left inside a gutted warehouse, lets out long cries. The kittens inch to the edge of the factory, their little paws almost touching this new lake that has appeared out of nowhere, each young animal wanting only to be back with its mother. But the adult cat will not risk swimming to her kittens, and the kittens cannot force themselves to step into this world of water that they know nothing about, no matter how much they want to suckle and be comforted and warm. The only thing they can do is cry.

Morgan closes the door and returns to her Blocks. She knows suffering is everywhere, that life was like this before the Great De-evolution and will continue to be this way after she is no longer here. But to see the suffering, to see animals, her and her Blocks included, that want nothing more than to get along as best as they can, only to be tormented by loss and anguish, is too much sometimes.

Maybe life begins the first time you understand the magnitude of suffering around you, and ends the last time you witness that sorrow.

It has only stopped raining for an hour before drops of water begin tinkling against the metal roof once again. Another storm already. And within seconds of those first drops, another barrage begins pouring down on the city. She does everything she can to get the thought of that cat and her kittens out of her mind. The worst part will be in the morning when the meowing has stopped and she knows the mother cat had to leave her kittens to die. That's exactly why she shouldn't have looked out the window in the first place.

"You're a trooper," she tells one of her resilient Blocks, patting him on the shoulder.

To another, she says, "I'm glad you're still here with me," and lets her hand brush over the woman's shin as she walks past.

Everywhere she goes, she tells each person how glad she is to have them around. But no amount of endless banter with her Blocks can get the sound of those sad cats out of her head.

The rain keeps falling.

32

She blinks back into consciousness, realizing she must have been asleep. It's the middle of the night. She knows this without looking at her alarm clock because the moon is past the highest set of windows in the top corner of the gymnasium. In a couple of hours the sun will be making its way across the horizon.

When she awakes in the morning, she rubs the sleep away from her eyes, moves out of bed, slowly, gauging what part of her body may not want to move that day. There is a sense of resigned determination at how the day must be spent. But every time she wakes in the middle of the night, she is immediately scared. Her jaw is clenched. Her eyes have a panicked intensity.

For once, her body is not sore. And this is one of the indicators she has learned that tells her if she is dreaming or if she is awake; ironically, it's only in her nightmares that her body doesn't feel like it's approaching one hundred years of life. Knowing she is dreaming does not keep the fear from descending upon her. She waits for a voice to call out from across the room and threaten her. Her heart quickens. She looks for a shadow moving toward her in the dark. Her head is throbbing.

Her eyes settle on Rachel, her veterinarian Block in

quadrant 3. She is sitting up in bed, staring directly at Morgan. The first instinct that crosses Morgan's mind is to tell Rachel that she is doing her best, that it wasn't her fault she got sick and so many Blocks died. No words arrive, though. She is mute again. Her body won't obey any of her commands. This is why she is terrified.

How long has Rachel been staring at her? Why, she wonders, do the Blocks, when they gaze at her, have such hatred in their eyes? Isn't it obvious that she is trying her best? For God's sake, she nearly died in her bed just a few days ago. What else can she do? She doesn't want to be remembered as a mass murderer. Can't they see that everything she has done has been with good intentions? She has never wanted to hurt anyone.

Rachel's eyes tell her that anything she might say to defend herself is pointless. The way the two pupils stare her down tells Morgan just how meaningless her life is to this Block. Less than meaningless. Worthless. The eyes say everything. If Morgan needed help, Rachel wouldn't be there to provide it. The vet spent her entire life caring for animals abandoned by owners migrating south, but she won't waste any concern on a piece of trash like Morgan. Never before have a pair of eyes shown such hatred.

She wants to ask Rachel why such hostility exists. If she is given a chance to explain herself, she is sure Rachel will understand. After all, Morgan spends part of each day refilling Rachel's nutrient bag and cleaning up after her. The Blocks she has had to transport to the incinerator were sent there just so people like Rachel can keep living. Words would make everything better. But she cannot speak.

Please don't hurt me, she begs to no one but herself. If she could, she would yell the words so they echoed to every living thing in Miami.

Rachel glances left. Looks right.

She isn't looking for witnesses, Morgan thinks. *She's looking for a weapon. She's looking for something to cut me with, something to beat me with.*

The possibilities are endless. Even in something as vapid as a group home for Blocks, there are countless ways to murder someone. Rachel could use something as simple as Morgan's own pillow to smother her. Unable to move, to defend herself, there's nothing Morgan would be able to do but hope she dies fairly quickly. Or maybe Rachel would take a washrag and force it down Morgan's throat until she's gagging on her own vomit. Maybe Rachel will fill a nutrient bag with cleaning chemicals and let Morgan feed off of it until her organs shut down. The forklift, the very one Morgan uses to carry each Block to their cremation, might be used to run over both of Morgan's legs and arms. With all four extremities crushed, she would lie on the concrete, helpless, in agonizing pain, until she died.

There are so many ways she can kill me. Please, God, help me.

Rachel moves. It's a slight movement, barely noticeable in the dark. It looks as though one hand is by Rachel's neck, one finger extended. There it pauses. She is still staring, ruthlessly, at Morgan, still sitting on the edge of her cot thirty feet away from where Morgan is lying.

Is she holding a finger to motion for silence? Is she mocking me for not being able to scream? Is she telling me she's going to slash my throat?

She has no idea what the gesture is supposed to signify, but she can tell from its owner's eyes that it can't mean anything good.

Please stop, Morgan wants to scream, but no noise comes from her throat.

A series of clouds move in front of the moon and the room becomes even darker. Now Morgan can barely see Rachel at all, can barely make out her outline in the shadows.

Is she moving? Is she going to get up and come this way? Please, no.

She gasps for air. Just thinking about all the ways Rachel might kill her makes it difficult to breathe. Her chest is burning. She wants to yell, "I didn't want to hurt anyone. It kills me to do it." But there are no words.

In the shadows, it looks as though a big smile breaks across Rachel's face. She is taking delight in Morgan's helplessness. Maybe the veterinarian can see how badly Morgan wants to plead on her own behalf and likes seeing someone else vulnerable for a change. The coldness in those eyes! It's as if Lady Death herself is there, taking her time to enjoy the moment.

Please, no!

Her scream—there is one this time—is still echoing in the gym when her eyes fly open. Finally, she's awake. Rachel is lying on her cot, motionless, thirty feet away. Morgan's scream echoes back and forth from one wall to the other, as if it will never end.

"Please, no!" followed by a softer, "Please, no!" and then another, "Please, no!"

She cries into her pillow while the echo fades and she is left, once again, to the silence of the gymnasium.

33

Moving from cot to cot, she cannot help but wonder where all the souls have gone since the Great De-evolution started. Whatever people call it, their soul or their life energy or whatever, she is inclined to believe more exists of people than the little you can see of them. It isn't an issue of missing loved ones but of wondering what is in store for all of mankind, especially all the Blocks who populated the earth. What happens to their souls? She doesn't ask if they have souls, the way some clergymen did when the Great De-evolution began; she knows the only difference between herself and the people around her is that they cannot speak or move. In all other things they are the same. If she has a soul, they have souls, too. If she doesn't, neither do they.

Different people around the world believe—believed—in different things. This was obvious, even when she was young. But it wasn't until she went to college that she learned about other beliefs than the ones her parents had taught her. That was when she changed from automatically accepting what her parents said and learned to respect the unique beliefs each religion held sacred. It wasn't that she had thought other religions' ideas were silly prior to that, it was simply that she didn't know anything outside of her own sheltered life. Her professor reminded the class that the majority of his students only held their religious views because they had been taught to them at an early age.

As he walked the room, the professor said, "If you were born somewhere else in the world, you might believe that spirits are reborn over and over again, just as kids on the other side of the world might be attending a class similar to this and learn all the crazy things you believe. This doesn't make what they hold to be true any more or less correct than what you believe." Her professor smiled. "Just different."

Morgan didn't leave the class believing she would come back in her next life as a zebra or a bird. Nor did she come away believing there were a hundred different gods, a single god, or no god at all. She left the class understanding that any of it was possible. All she could be sure of were the things she saw and learned for herself. For everything else, for all the things she didn't know, how could she be so egotistical to think one thing was right and another thing wrong?

Sometimes, she finds herself walking amongst what is left of the group home's population, thinking about what it will be like to meet each of these Blocks in the next life and finally be able to experience them as normal people. Instead of pretending what Cindy and Irving and Algernon might have said, they would actually be able to speak to her.

And sometimes she thinks about how everyone might die and simply stop existing. The Blocks she has sent to the incinerator will never have a chance to hear her apologize for selecting them. Everything will go quiet. There won't be pain in hell or joy in heaven, there will only be an absence of everything. Their entire lives will have consisted of being motionless in bed until Morgan sent them to their deaths. Nothing else.

She is also fond of imagining her Blocks and herself as far-off animals in their next lives. Occasionally, instead of carrying on fictitious conversations with the men and women she looks after, expanding the story of their lives, she imagines them as reincarnated animals in the Serengeti or the

Amazon. She thinks of Richard, the grumpy pilot, as a snake, and Roger, the happy pilot, as a prairie dog. She thinks of Aristotle, her world traveler, as a dolphin, and Justin, her mountain climber, as a goat.

When she's in a particularly good mood, she imagines that all the Blocks in the world were people who reached enlightenment in their previous life. Her Blocks have never complained about anything. They have given up everything that could cause sorrow. Maybe the Blocks, she fancies, are those people who were more spiritual than everyone else and reached a higher consciousness. They are the ones who have reached nirvana.

"I like that thought," her Zen master Block says. "You know, desire is nothing but the search for pleasure, and fear is nothing but the memory of pain. Both lead to suffering. And the Blocks are free of both."

"Very true," she says.

But on the occasions when she is tired or can't stop coughing or is feeling sorry for herself, she thinks humanity was a waste, that people never came close to reaching the potential they were given. Surely, humans hadn't evolved enough if they spent thousands of years killing each other. What was the point of human invention and ingenuity if it only led to more brutal ways of killing someone or to the corrupt and ruthless ruling over everyone else with more efficiency?

Too many people spent their entire time on this planet living thoughtlessly, giving in to impulses without having a meaning to their lives. These are the times she thinks the Great De-evolution came about because humans were a failed creature. Everyone she once knew, all the spirits that were recycled for thousands of years, have one less species to inhabit now.

She has no idea what she really believes.

34

On her walk through the rows—she keeps forgetting she can no longer call them that; they are a mere splattering of dots—she breathes deeply, trying to take in the incense wafting through the air. After an hour of the little stick burning, sending its puffs of smoke every which way, she is able to convince herself that the smell of death and human waste are slowly drifting away. The entire gymnasium begins to smell like *Arabic Cinders* or *Ocean Salt* or whatever fragrance she picks for the day. Every corner of the enormous room must smell like a campfire in the desert or the mist coming in from the ocean. The smells were assigned names by random people decades earlier, but they still somehow seem to fit.

Taking in the flavorful smoke, she closes her eyes and imagines herself under a tarp so the sand doesn't get in her eyes, or with a blanket around her so the mist doesn't get her too wet. It's a nice thing to imagine. When *Bay of Bengal Breeze* is wafting through the gym, she imagines herself walking through an endless marketplace, baskets full of fish and herbs, instead of walking by what remains of the world's quiet population. When *Mount Everest Air* is sending little bits of smoke throughout the facility, rather than seeing herself surrounded by Blocks who are all as old as she is, she imagines herself amongst little Tibetan boys and girls, all eager to be old enough for the day that they too can attempt to climb the great mountain.

Her mood depends on how exhausted she is as she makes her way from cot to cot. The smells can make her feel like she is able to live out one tiny aspect of the world that not even mankind's extinction could take away from her. But they can also make her lonely, cause her to long for the days when a group of thirty caretakers would laugh and joke with each other as they replaced nutrient bags and changed bedding.

The incense belonged to a helper who passed away nearly ten years ago. Morgan uses the sweet-smelling sticks frugally because there aren't many left, and once they are gone another aspect of life will fade away. The food processor can do many things, but it can't make her anything resembling scented sticks to burn. Back when the processors were first distributed through the country, everyone took turns finding new codes and recipes to make items that the machine's creators hadn't intended. She can go online and find codes to make just about every over-the-counter medication and just about any illicit drug. Never, though, did anyone waste time trying to figure out if the machine could produce incense. Understandable, given how many more important things there were to think about in those days. But these little things are all she has left.

No one has arrived in Miami for twelve years. The final nomads have long since passed away. Family, everyone she has ever loved, is dead. Everything Stanley Steinbecker wrote about in *Mapping the Great De-evolution*, the nonfiction account of how one sociologist thought the declining population would play out, has already happened. His last chapter, about the world's last people, about even the final settlements becoming ghost towns, has already come to fruition. And yet, she is still here. Leave it to Morgan, the last of the last, to live past what even Steinbecker could foresee. Leave it to her to live through the unwritten chapter, after everyone else has passed away and not a single other person is there to offer support, not even on the other side of the world. She has thought of trying to write her own chapter to his book, an addendum to the last New York Times Bestseller ever published, a chapter which summarizes the little things that not even a sociologist could fathom: rows of Blocks dying when the only living caretaker falls ill, the way her music echoes through the empty gymnasium, and yes, even the last sticks of incense.

By the time the final bit of the wood burns to ash, she is done caring for twelve of her sixteen Blocks. It makes her happy, though, that the smell lingers the rest of the day. Even at seven o'clock, as the black of night begins to creep through the rafters, the smell of *Turkish Wood* still floats in the air.

She imagines walking the streets of Istanbul, even though she really has no idea what the city is like—was like, when people still lived there—and, discouraged, realizes, her mental Istanbul is the same as her mental Bangladesh and her mental Budapest. They are all the same place in her daydreams because she never got to see them and distinguish them for herself.

For the duration of her life, the majority of the earth's wonders have been accessible to her only in pictures. It is impossible for this realization not to upset her. As the odor dissipates, her chest feels heavy and she cannot help but feel like the smell might as well have been named *Smell 237* or *Smell 4-F6* because random laboratory names mean as much to her as any far-off land's name. And she resents ever finding pleasure in a smell just because it's different than the smell she has to breathe every other day.

None of her Blocks care what the gymnasium smells like anyway. Why should she? They all probably think she is crazy for burning the scented sticks of wood in the first place. With three-quarters of her Blocks dead, she finally has time to slow down, can finally finish her chores at a reasonable hour. And what does she do? She doesn't cook herself a grand meal. She doesn't go for a walk in the neighborhood. No, she burns a stick of wood and makes herself sad.

"You can't keep doing this to yourself."

She turns and looks behind her to see who has said this. Gault, her mad scientist, the one who tried to cause chaos during the end of the world, is lying there.

She tries to smile, says, "You know I'm one step away from madness when an evil mastermind is concerned about me."

With his feelings hurt, he doesn't offer a reply. Probably, he is plotting how to blow the entire group home to smithereens.

When she sleeps that night, her dreams are fitful. She wakes in a sweat, gasping for air, but cannot remember what the dream was about. Her clock tells her it's the middle of the night. There are still another three hours of possible sleep remaining if she wants it.

Please don't let the nightmare start right back up.

She closes her eyes again.

35

However, the nightmare, or a similar one, does continue. And as the dreams have progressed—from an initial unidentified Block watching her in the night, to one staring at her, to one gesturing toward her—the pattern of what occurs is part of what she dreads: they are getting closer. They will continue to approach until they are close enough to do to her as she has done to them.

Why is it never the Blocks who have a right to be upset with her that haunt her nightmares? Why is it always the living? Part of her thinks the nightmares would terrify her less if they at least featured people who should rightfully be seeking revenge. At least that would make sense. At least that would give the episodes a purpose that could be explained away. But having Blocks appear whom she still cares for each day, who should be grateful to her, who have no reason to despise her, makes her even more anxious.

Her first thought after each dream is always, *Am I making the wrong decisions? I must be doing something wrong.*

She goes through the rest of her day trying to figure out where she could have done things differently. Surely, the Blocks would not be haunting her if she were doing what she was supposed to be doing. People don't seek revenge without having a reason. By its very definition, revenge requires that she do some amount of wrong before they come to get their recompense.

The Block in this nightmare is Coelho, her Zen master. As she watches, Coelho's head turns and stares at her. He props himself on one elbow, then looks directly into her eyes.

It's okay, Morgan thinks. *He would never hurt me. Not my Zen master.*

So relieved is she by the identity of the man who occupies this night's dream that she actually lets out a sigh. But her Zen master's eyes narrow when she does this. Her comfort agitates him. There is nothing Zen-like about him in her dream, nothing peaceful. Even his breathing, usually calm and steady, becomes a series of angry huffs though his nose. Just looking at her is enough for him to forget who he is, for him to give up his tranquil nature. The same man who wouldn't hurt an insect wants to see her dead.

Coelho doesn't waste time putting his hand to his own neck to let her know strangulation is in her near future. Nor does he run his thumb from one side of his neck to the other to let her know how soon it will be until a dull knife is tearing chunks of flesh away from her throat. There is none of this.

Morgan has the gall to think, *Well, this dream won't be too bad then.*

Just as this thought enters her mind, she gasps. Coelho is getting off the bed. He is coming toward her. Slowly, as if unsure of his balance after being motionless on the mattress for so long, the Zen master lets one leg hang off the side of his bed, then the other.

She wants to yell at him that he has no reason to be angry with her, wants to tell him that she is doing the best she can. But of course not a single muscle will move, not even in her throat.

Once both feet are touching the floor, Coelho uses an elbow to push himself into a seated position so he is facing her. He doesn't pause on the edge of the cot to threaten her, to growl, or to look for a weapon. These are all wastes of time compared to actually closing the distance between them and doing what all the other Blocks have merely threatened. Immediately, one foot moves ahead of the other, only inches, but enough to let her know he is coming in her direction.

And like that, Coelho is standing. His left foot creeps toward her. Then his right foot.

No matter how hard she tries to scream, no sound will come. Not even a gurgle or a groan. She tries to push herself off the bed so she can run and get away from him, but none of her muscles respond.

The Zen master's feet shuffle closer to her. He is only thirty feet away. Now twenty-eight feet. His toenails, long and curled, scuff against the floor each time he takes a small step toward her. Twenty-six feet.

He's going to kill me.

By now, she has witnessed all too frequently that what happens in her dreams happens in real life. This means that when Coelho chokes her to death in her nightmare…

He's going to come over here and kill me.

Any comfort in knowing this is a dream has completely vanished.

She stares into his eyes. Usually, they are at peace. If the eyes are the gateway to the soul, Coelho's usually reveal a soul who has found answers to all the important questions in life. But now, the eyes are different. They don't sparkle. They are unflinching. They want blood. They want her to cry. And they never deviate from her, not even for a moment. He doesn't look down to make sure the path is clear or to aid his balance after walking for the first time in all his life. He only stares right into her, cruelly, as if to let her know he may not have decided yet just how, exactly, she will die—maybe by being starved to death; maybe from blood loss after pricking her with a pin thousands of times and watching little drops of blood form from each of unseen hole in her old body. No matter what, though, she will be dying very soon.

One foot shuffles in front of the other—a patient

zombie. Another foot closer.

He's going to cut my ears off, sew my eyelids shut, put a gag in my mouth. He's going to show me what it's like to be a Block, to be helpless.

If she could yell just once, he would blink back into being the Zen master she knows. He would see how wrong this all is. Surely, he would know she hasn't done anything wrong. Why can't she scream?

Instead, she is crying. Tears pour from both eyes, streaming down her cheeks and onto her pillow.

Coelho's feet shuffle closer. He is half the way to her now.

He wants me to be like him. He's going to stick a pin in my ears and burst my eardrums so I go deaf. He's going to force a spoon behind my eyes and pop them from the sockets so I go blind. He's going to pull my tongue out, right as I watch, so I go mute. Please, no.

But if Coelho can hear her thoughts, he is not letting on. She cries and cries.

Another foot closer.

Her eyes burst open. Immediately, she darts upright and looks at Coelho lying motionless on his bed. Her face and pillow are soaked. Tears. Her throat is sore as if she has been yelling all the things she wished she could have screamed in her nightmare. Falling back on her bed, her neck is cold against the wet pillowcase. All she can do is sob.

"Even you, Coelho?" she says, unable to believe a man devoted to a spiritual life could be as brutally cold as he had just appeared to be in her dream.

Coelho does not reply. He, like all the Blocks around him, is asleep. Only Morgan is awake. Only Morgan is shaking and crying as the air conditioner kicks back on again.

36

Except for the continuing nightmares, the days following her illness are fairly pleasant ones. She is able to get through the chores each day while there is still sunlight out. This affords her a chance to step outside without the guilt of knowing someone is starving or sitting in filth and will be doing so until she returns to finish her list of duties.

The various oranges and reds that comprise the Florida sunsets always amaze her. The sky's fiery colors take her back, so many years earlier, to the Grand Canyon. If there is a heaven, for her at least, it would have to combine the Florida sunset with the Grand Canyon's rocks. Everything in front of her would glow like warm embers. The sky, the earth, everything.

Only one Block has died in the week since her illness and the mass of casualties that resulted from it. This one, Elaine had named him Clark, died from what Morgan diagnoses simply as "old age." One day he was alive, seemingly healthy, and the next day he wasn't breathing. At their age, with the human population coming to an end, it's something she has had to witness more than any battlefield nurse or medic ever did. She has seen more death than a black-masked hangman or an executioner's axe.

Clark's death, while unfortunate, does not leave her in

a somber mood the way she is each time she has to sacrifice someone from the group. This death was just part of life, the same as if she witnessed someone pass away in a hospital bed, without pain, after having a chance to say goodbye to their family and friends. She can deal with that.

An odd thing begins to happen, though: after days of having more time to herself, she finds herself resenting the hours she has to spend caring for the Blocks.

There are almost no other options for what she could be doing with her time. She knows this. Yet, a part of her resents that this is a situation she is forced into rather than one she chooses. If she is going to miss the sun rise each morning, if she is going to feel obligated to work nonstop each day until the very last Block is clean and has a full nutrient bag, she would like to think it's because she has the option of not being there. Obviously, it's physically possible for her to open the gymnasium door and walk away from the men and women who need her care, but it isn't an idea she can entertain. The thought is so ugly to her that it makes her groan the way her mother used to when she had to step on a spider. She might as well be a prisoner within the gym. The doors might as well be padlocked from the outside, the windows sealed with chains or boarded shut.

As she makes her way from cot to cot, performing the same actions she performs every single day of every week of every year, she grumbles to herself.

"Don't look at me," one of her grouchier Blocks says to her. "I like being taken care of as much as you like caring for me."

She doesn't say anything, doesn't entertain this Block's self-pity. She moves to the next cot, to a college professor who specialized in the history and effects of the Great De-evolution, who has never been anything but pleasant and agreeable, even during the worst of times.

But the grumpy Block calls after her: "Do you think I want to be stuck in this bed? Do you think I wanted my whole life to be like this? You have an entire world available to you that I don't have, and here you are feeling sorry for yourself."

She looks to the congenial former professor for help, maybe just a subtle reaffirmation that Morgan shouldn't listen to the taunts of the irascible Block two cots over, but the professor only stares happily at the ceiling until Morgan repositions her. No defense is offered on her behalf. No words are uttered to reassure Morgan that the grumpy Block might just be having a bad day and shouldn't be listened to.

"You seem unhappy."

She turns and sees her Zen master, Coelho. As opposed to the Zen master who visited her in her nightmare, this Coelho has always been understanding, has never held a judgment against her.

"Yeah, you could say that."

"You carry a heavy burden."

"That's very true," she says.

"You know, desire is the cause of all unhappiness."

"I desire not to have to care for all of you for the rest of my life."

"Touché," the Zen master says.

She goes about cleaning one of the other Blocks in silence before looking back at him again.

"Tell me something, Coelho."

"Anything."

"Why did you come after me in my nightmare? I thought you were different from the others."

"Different? How?"

"I thought you had everything figured out. I thought you knew true peace."

"But, Morgan, I am only what you make of me."

She is irritated by this type of response. She knows each Block is only what they are because she and Elaine assigned lives to them. It does no good to remind her of this, only exasperates her.

Coelho seems to understand how she interpreted his answer: "That is not what I meant, Morgan. What I mean is, who am I to say I am a Zen master or just some guy looking for answers? Who is to say Gault is an evil mastermind or just an unhappy soul? Who is to say any of this?"

She doesn't know what kind of answer he is looking for, and so she says nothing.

"It is only you," he says. "We are what you think we are. And not because we are Blocks. Elaine is as you remember her. If you remembered her differently, she would be different. Your reality determines everything. It is only because you think of me as a so-called Zen master that you think I should have these answers you speak of. If you didn't respect what I said, well then maybe I wouldn't be so wise after all. The same goes for how you think of yourself, the people around you, your actions. Everything."

"Thank you, Coelho."

"I only tell you what you already know. You had only forgotten, and I merely reminded you."

"What's going to happen when one of the Blocks gets their hands on me in my nightmare? Will I die in real life?"

"Not even the wisest man knows the future."

"Coelho?"

"Yes, Morgan?"

"Why haven't you answered my original question?"

"Which was?"

"Why were you in my dream?"

"Your reality determines everything. I did not come to you in your dream; you brought me there. If you hadn't wanted me there, truly, I wouldn't have been."

"Do you really think I would want you to appear in my nightmares just so you can torture me?"

But Coelho doesn't have anything else to say for the evening, and so Morgan moves on to the next bed.

37

The things she longs for these days, as an old woman, would make the teenage version of herself burst out laughing. She dreams of having a day without chores so she can watch the sun rise, watch its progress in the sky all day, and, finally, watch it set. All without worrying about anything else. Even in her fantasy, the idea that she could somehow be free of all responsibility just for one day, and just so she can watch the way the sun changes the appearance of the city's skyline, seems absolutely ludicrous, like winning the lottery or finding a magic genie. But now, with only fifteen Blocks to care for, she at least has enough free time to see the sun as it comes up over the ocean and watch it again as it sets behind the gymnasium.

Maybe life starts with your first fantasy, ends with your last fantasy, and is measured by all of the hopes and dreams in between.

The glowing EXIT sign shows her where a different world can be found. She goes to the door there and pushes, but it doesn't budge. It takes her entire weight against the metal door for it to open. Sun bursts forth. Her hand goes in front of her eyes, forcing her to squint. For once, it's not pouring outside. It's the same sun she has seen all of her life, but after being indoors for so long, she is mesmerized by it all over again.

All of life, everything on Earth, has been made possible because of that orange circle in the sky. That should never be taken for granted. But sadly, it is. The lights above her in the group home have become her norm. So used to experiencing only two levels of light these days—the yellow glow from the florescent bulbs above her, and the pitch black of night—she almost cries at the sight of the sun again. The light makes her squint, but she craves it.

The city calls to her. It's overgrown with trees and weeds where streets used to be. It resembles a rainforest in which someone tried their best to erect a city. And yet it calls to her. She shuffles forward, only a couple of feet closer, toward the remnants of high-rises and parks, enough to satisfy a tiny part of her desire to see the bustling city she once knew.

With the hinge pulling it closed, the door slams shut behind her. It is solid, heavy. A loud bang startles the surrounding birds into flight. The sky is filled with black dots as they retreat to some other forgotten city.

Cursing herself for craving a glimpse of the city, she shuffles back to the door. It's locked. As much as she pulls on it, even with all of her weight, the door doesn't budge. With the sound of one door slamming, she has gone from being mesmerized by the sun and the light to realizing she is separated from the people who need her care.

Banging on the door is useless. No one on the other side can let her back in. The Blocks will not magically awaken just to preserve themselves and excuse their caretaker for her mistake. She bangs on the door anyway. But at her age, with barely enough strength to reposition a deathly thin mannequin lying on a cot, her fists cause nothing more than gentle clacks against the thick metal.

There are doors to the gymnasium on two other sides of the building. There is still hope. Walking through tall grass where the sidewalk used to be, around the side of the facility, she sees the overhang where some of the caretakers used to read books during their breaks and where others waited for phone calls from family members migrating south. Three bird's nests exist where the overhang is pulling away from the brick wall. On the ground, a cat, too thin, only fur and bones, looks up at the nests, waiting patiently in hopes that the wind will knock an egg to the ground. So hungry is it that it ignores this strange old woman walking near it.

Just beyond the overhang, she finds the side doors. They are locked too. The windows are too high to reach, and even if she could reach them, she doesn't have the strength to lift herself up or pull herself through the opening. Even when she was seventy that would have been a task above her capability.

Standing there, looking at the building where almost three quarters of her life have been spent walking back and forth in the same room, caring for the same people, she thinks about what else she can possibly do. If there is a large truck nearby, maybe she can drive it into one of the exterior walls and create her own opening in the brick. But she knows this is wishful thinking. More likely, she will be killed when the truck drives head-on into the barrier.

Even if she does survive, the new opening can't be sealed once she knocks down part of the wall. She has all the extra sets of bed sheets she could ever want, but they will not keep the wildlife outside. Rats and crows will flood the group home. The next day, during her rounds, her Blocks would have rodents scurrying on their chests and faces, little pockets of flesh eaten away from the people she has spent her life caring for where the disease-ridden pests have feasted. Vultures would tear juicy eyeballs out of their sockets, would dine on the Blocks' tongues after ripping them away.

She turns her back on the building, tries to make herself simply walk away from it and from her Blocks. If she does, she can spend each day in quiet. Get up whenever she wants. Nap whenever she wants. Worry about only bathing herself and no one else. Keep herself healthy. But she cannot do this. She cannot walk away.

It's pointless to do so, but she hobbles as quickly as she can back to the very door she exited from and bangs on the metal again. As her little hands hit the door, she begins to yell for someone to let her back inside.

"I'm sorry," she screams to her Blocks on the other side of the door, each waiting for care that will never arrive. "I'm sorry. I've messed up so badly."

She is crying now. Her Blocks will all starve to death because she wanted to reminisce about a city that hasn't existed in decades. Her wrinkled hands bang against the door with no results.

"Please, somebody let me in. Please." She screams this through her sobbing.

She awakes back in the group home. The sky is black. The sun is gone. Rain patters against the metal roof. Her mouth is open. She was in the middle of a scream in her nightmare, and the echo lets her know she was screaming in her sleep as well. If a tape recorder were there, next to her pillow, it would have recorded her yelling in her sleep, "Please, somebody let me in. Please."

Her hands are curled into balls as if they had been lashing out at the door she saw in her nightmare. Her face is covered in tears.

It's only four o'clock in the morning, but she gets out of bed and begins her chores anyway. If she gets an early enough start to her day, she can eat dinner outside on the steps while it's still sunny. This is the goal she has in mind for herself: eating a meal out in the fresh air, the sun shining down on her, reminding her that there is still life everywhere, even when it seems like there isn't.

She uses this goal to get herself through the day, but she can't help but think, as the hours go by, that she is being punished. This was the first dream she has had that doesn't involve the Blocks coming to kill her, and instead it has her accidentally abandoning them and realizing, with its own special kind of terror, that leaving them is just as scary as seeing them move toward her in the middle of the night. One nightmare is exchanged for another.

That's what I get for complaining to Coelho.

She cleans the remaining fifteen Blocks. Refills their nutrient bags. Repositions them. At the end of her chores, it is still light out, and there is enough time to make a meal and eat it outside.

Just remember to get a doorstop so I'm not locked out, she thinks, carrying a plate with her to the exit.

38

Her parents believed everything has a reason and a purpose. They raised Morgan to believe the same thing. Birds, they said, kept the insect population in balance and helped flowers and plants spread into new areas. Flowers exist to give bugs food. Without one piece of the cycle, the entire process falls apart. Everything has a purpose and things exist to serve that purpose. They smiled as they told their daughter she also had a purpose—she just had to find what it was. They made this declaration with a grin, as if it wasn't absolutely horrifying for a little girl to hear these types of things. What child wants the pressure of knowing they exist for a single reason and it's up to them to find it?

She grew up wondering what her purpose could be. Even after ninety-three years of life, she still wonders. Is it still to come? Has it already passed and she missed what it was? Maybe her purpose became voided when the Great De-evolution started; the thing she was supposed to do disappeared from the realm of possibility when people who couldn't move or talk were all that could be born. A scientist? A teacher? Perhaps she and the other regular people born just before her, the last generation, had a different course lined up for their lives, but because Blocks replaced normal people all of those purposes vanished. Maybe Morgan was meant to be a doctor and help cure the sick. Maybe she was supposed to be a politician and help lead her country. Or be a lawyer and free wrongly convicted people from jail. Or be a journalist and expose some great fraud. Or maybe give birth to children that would one day accomplish these things.

All of these possibilities vanished before she was even old enough to understand they had ever existed. Instead of her mom asking her what she wanted to be when she grew up, her mom looked sad and said she had no idea what the future would hold. This was back when lawyers had stopped taking new clients, politicians were disappearing in the night, and doctors were closing their practices to move south with their families.

Instead of being told she could be an astronaut or President of the United States or anything else she wanted, her father told her that an entire new set of possibilities would be created due to the changing world. He didn't know, though, what those possibilities were. Looking back, she thinks he was just trying to be optimistic. Probably, he wouldn't have mentioned anything about new options if he knew schools were going to be turned into food processor factories and power generator assembly lines.

As she walks amongst her Blocks, she finds herself wondering if she was born just so she could take care of these people at the end of their lives. Is she on this earth just to provide for people who can't take care of themselves? She has never had kids. She never saved someone's life or inspired someone to do something greater with their time on this planet. She never, really, did anything except grow up from being a kid to an adult, move south with her parents, and then begin watching over these people. Was that her purpose: to have a normal life before caring for the bodies all around her?

What kind of purpose is that? she thinks.

Maybe she never had a set expectation at all. Her parents were just being encouraging, or were just plain wrong. There was never any grand scheme in the universe for what she would do. She was born one day and it was up to her to create the life she wanted and to avoid the life she didn't want. There is no destiny guiding her life, no predetermined ending.

Back when she was younger, healthier, and had help taking care of all the Blocks residing in this home, she went through a phase when the only books she would read were real-life accounts of people surviving disasters. This was, of course, to help her decide if her life was one of free will or if it had a predestined course.

She read about a man who drifted at sea for nine months, living off nothing but rainwater and raw fish. She read about a small group of men who journeyed across the Gobi Desert without any supplies. One book told about a woman who survived in the frozen wilderness for two weeks, the lone survivor of a plane crash. And another told of a man who should have frozen to death on Mount Everest but who survived with only minor frostbite. Her hope was that these accounts would convince her whether survivors lived because they were destined to live, or if they had made their own fate. Was she living in this group home, only a few years short of one hundred, the last woman in the world, because she created this outcome for herself, or was it nothing more than luck and happenstance?

The stack of books did not help. Half of the survivors came away feeling like they had not only survived the disaster, but had also experienced it in the first place, because God had a plan for them. The other half felt like life and death were nothing but a pair of dice cast without their having any say in the roll. They had lived while their loved ones had died because they simply refused to give up, not because God had chosen one instead of the other. She finished the books with no more or less of an answer than she had started with. Was she merely drifting through life or was she being guided?

Was the weather a hint? She can't decide if the hurricanes barely missing Miami are a sign that she is lucky or that God is protecting her. Probably, it's a matter of time until a storm hits squarely on top of their group home. She tried to find a message in the eyes of the Blocks, both the ones she still cares for and the many she had to sacrifice for the benefit of the group, but she couldn't tell if their silence was to force her into figuring out God's plan for herself, or if there was nothing to figure out at all. Maybe silence is just silence.

She is sure, though, beyond all doubt, of one thing: she was not created just to be the final living person at the final settlement. There has to be a better reason. Whether it's God or destiny or happenstance or whatever else might be guiding her life, she is sure she was not put on this earth just to be the last person at the end of everything. It's a coincidence that she is here instead of Elaine. It's mere chance that she is alive after Daniel grew old and passed away.

But what a coincidence that is... some might even call it miraculous. A great sigh comes from her throat.

She will never be able to decide if she has a purpose in life, and if she does, if this is it, or if it was something else that has already passed her by.

39

Gault is already halfway across the room when Morgan opens her eyes. She doesn't know how long it has taken the mad scientist to move all the way from the end of quadrant 3 to where he is now at quadrant 1, but his look is the same as all the other Blocks that have come for her in her sleep: he doesn't smile or frown, he doesn't blink.

The eyes say everything: *My dear lady, I am coming to kill you. When I get my hands around your lovely neck, you will know what it's like to be helpless. You're going to wish you were already dead.*

Is this her punishment for taking someone else's life? Maybe it doesn't make any difference why she sends a Block to the incinerator; any death is wrong even if it's to help everyone else. She is only trying to ease everyone's suffering. Why can't they see that? As Gault's feet shuffle across the room, she thinks maybe it doesn't matter if killing someone will ease the lives of ten other people or a thousand; if something is wrong, nothing will make it right. She's just a normal person, why did she think she was qualified to pass judgment on who should live and who should die?

Gault's feet grind against the concrete floor as they make their tortoise-like progress in her direction.

My lady, he is thinking. *I'll show you how to kill someone properly. I'm going to laugh as you wither away. When you cry for me to put you out of your misery, I'm going to stand over you and applaud.*

She is used to the routine of being paralyzed in her sleep, knows there is nothing her body can do except lie there, and yet her mind screams for her to get up and flee for safety.

Gault is amused by this idea. She can tell what he is thinking: *It's funny, really. I always thought I was meant to destroy the world, not act as the angel of vengeance on someone else taking the very lives I had planned on taking. Our world certainly is ironic, my dear.*

His feet inch closer. Gault offers her a smile.

You may think you can die with dignity. You can't, though. Maybe you think you won't be conscious of your misery because your body will go into shock. This is not true. I promise you that you'll suffer. That, my lady, is a guarantee.

He's another foot closer. His hand inches toward Morgan, as if he can't wait to strangle her.

She is conscious that this is only a dream. She understands that in real life she is not a Block, knows Gault is lying on his bed. However, this knowledge doesn't help keep the terror away. Whatever happens in her nightmare will happen in real life. To date, that has only meant screaming herself awake, clawing at her blanket, and crying onto her pillow. But if Gault strangles her to death in her nightmare, Morgan will die, right in her own bed, from suffocation. If he lets battery acid trickle down the back of her throat, Morgan's kidneys and liver will shut down before her heart does the same. This is true. She has seen all too many times how her body reacts to her dreams to doubt it. No matter what happens, when he finally imposes his judgment upon her, Morgan will never wake up.

His feet shuffle forward.

If only she could make her tongue listen to her and form words, she would plead, "Please understand. I'm only trying to take care of all of you the best I can. This is a situation I never wanted to be in. Surely you can see how all of you would have suffered if I tried to take care of everyone. I can only do so much. Why can't you see that?"

But no words will come out. She can't even crawl away. Her body is motionless as her mind screams to run.

Gault inches closer. He is almost close enough to extend his arm and take hold of her. His eyes glitter. They tell of all the horrid things he will do to her once he is at her side.

You will beg me to let you die. You may not believe in hell right now, but you will.

Morgan wants to push this evil away, wants to squeeze her eyes shut so it will all disappear. Not even her eyes obey her. She tries to squeeze them shut, but no matter how hard she tries, she can see him approaching. Each time he shuffles forward, his clothes, too baggy for his slender frame, drift about as if being carried in a current of water.

With her eyes still closed, she wakes up. She is conscious, even with her eyelids squeezing shut as hard as she can, that the nightmare is over. Gault will be back in his bed. She relaxes. When her eyelids flutter open, it's just as she thought it would be: the mad scientist is across the room on his cot, back in the area that used to be quadrant 3.

If the glass is half full, at least she only has dreams in which she screams or makes a fist or closes her eyes. If she has a nightmare in which she claws her face off, she would awaken with blood running down her face and skin stuck between her fingernails. If she has a nightmare in which she bites off her tongue, she would wake up unable to form half the alphabet, the bloody stump of her tongue laying on the pillow next to her face.

If Gault did starve her, would her organs shut down from not receiving enough nourishment? If a Block beats her with his fists, will Morgan die with her eyes swollen shut and her nose broken? If a Block slits her throat, will she choke to death on her own blood?

With a sigh, she rolls out of bed and begins her day. The clock says it's four in the morning, but it's better to start moving than to stay in bed and think about never waking up again.

40

How can it rain so much? She is sure, given time, Miami and the entire East Coast will be under water. If there were still kids around, it wouldn't be long before they had to abandon the places she once thought of as beach towns. Pittsburgh, Charlotte, and Atlanta would be the new places to lie out on the sand and watch the waves. That is what the endless rain tells her.

Even on the days when the previous storm has passed, she looks outside to see nothing but flooded roads. Not even the weeds and bushes that have covered every part of the sidewalks and streets are visible anymore until the water begins to recede and their green tops begin to poke from the water's surface. Will New York and Baltimore and Washington DC, and everywhere all the way down to Miami, become lost cities under the water? When the next creatures with higher intelligence appear on earth, will they notice the tops of skyscrapers poking out of the ocean and, upon exploring them, discover that an entire system of roads and tunnels exists beneath the water as well? Is that how Japan's underwater ruins came into existence? Will our great cities come to the same end?

"Awful weather for running."

Morgan looks down at the Block in front of her. Erin

was her Block who liked running ultra marathons.

She tells Morgan, "The winter cold and the summer heat never bothered me, but running in the wind and rain really sucked."

"I can imagine."

It has been a long time since Erin ran one of her marathons. As the Great De-evolution progressed, they were one of the first forms of recreation to fade away. It takes long stretches of wilderness to put the runner's heart at peace—no one in their right mind would run on a treadmill for a hundred miles—but it was this same wilderness, much of it having been returned to the animals, which kept the runners indoors.

People thought it was odd at first when one of the runners in her marathon started the race but never showed up at the finish line. It wasn't until this happened a second and then a third time that people realized wolves and wild dogs were dragging runners off the trails and eating them.

Erin's running shoes had to be put away. The only thing she has now are the memories of when her feet used to carry her for miles and miles, never more at peace with herself than when passing by long stretches of farmland and forest.

"It's okay," Erin says. "The memories of those days will never fade away."

Erin's eyes have a permanent grace about them that makes it look as though everything happening in the world is slightly amusing to her, is all part of a plan that, while unknown to her, is always fun to watch unfold.

She handled the changes that came about during the Great De-evolution a lot better than most people. It was easy, back in those days, for people to panic as the first parts of their culture began to disappear. Everyone still had long lives ahead of them, but it didn't feel that way sometimes.

Erin has always seemed a little younger than the other bodies around her, a little more carefree. Maybe that is what a sense of freedom in the wilderness does for you. Elaine had once predicted that Erin would be the last remaining Block because of how youthful she seemed to be. Morgan refrained from guessing which Block might last the longest because it seemed rude to all the others. This, of course, had just brought about another round of groans from her friend.

After finishing caring for Erin, Morgan pats her runner on the arm and moves to the next bed. For the rest of the night, she finds herself thinking about one thing she has lost over the years that she wishes she could get back, her equivalent to the yearning Erin will always have for running. She thinks of the park, from back when she used to live with her parents, and how it was always packed with fields of flowers. She thinks of staying up at night with her friends and seeing all the stars littering the night sky.

But that isn't the first thing that pops into her head. Her very first vision is of the Grand Canyon. There is nothing more beautiful in the world. When one of her Blocks says life is only what you see, she thinks of the hidden power in that vast gash of land. When one of them says the world is ruled by mathematics and science, she thinks of the pure chaos in those rocks.

She will never get back there, she knows that. But are the memories of that place really enough to keep her going each day? Is the memory of red rock merging with yellow sky and orange sun really enough to give her peace of mind? Just knowing it's out there, just knowing she had been there once, a long time ago. Is that enough?

"Trust me, it is," Erin calls out, but Morgan puts her head down and closes her eyes without replying.

41

It's easy to imagine all the things she might have done through her lifetime if the Great De-evolution had never happened. Backpacking across Europe. Falling in love. Having her heart broken and then finding a way to trust again before eventually falling hopelessly in love a second time. Perhaps children. Maybe even living much of her life on a different continent. These things are the essence of daydreaming, and she is not immune to all the what-ifs. It would be a fair bet to guess all of the other caretakers also had these same hopes and dreams. Probably, she thinks, everyone who lived through the Great De-evolution lived an entire life of would-have-beens, could-have-beens, should-have-beens.

Not so easy is imagining what her life would be like at her current age if the Blocks had never spelled mankind's exit. When she was young, she never imagined herself as an extremely old woman. Married—she imagined that. Living in the French or Italian countryside—she imagined that, too. She even pictured what it would be like to become a grandmother. That wasn't easy, but she started by envisioning her own grandmother and how happy she had been to have guests, or how she never seemed to notice all the times Morgan was a bratty girl, the way all little kids can be brats when they have to visit relatives instead of getting to play with their friends.

But her own grandmother died at the age of seventy-six, when Morgan was only twelve. Morgan has exceeded that life by seventeen years. And no part of those seventeen years or any of the ones preceding them involved visits from out of town relatives. She tries to envision her grandmother being much older, removes the expectation of any more guests. This is how she tries to imagine what her life would be like now, if she didn't have a gymnasium of Blocks to care for.

What she comes away with is an old woman standing around looking out the window, waiting for something, anything, to happen. Maybe, if the Great De-evolution had never occurred, she would be in an old age home, surrounded by other senior citizens. She would get a chance to be the one being cared for by younger, healthier men and women. And in her own way, she would be treated as though she were a Block by those caretakers who were too young to realize they would be feeble one day as well.

The idea of being cared for instead of doing the caring is so foreign to her that it's easier to imagine the Blocks becoming normal people, and imagining herself as one of the workers at the old-age home, where she still provides them with care, than it is for her to take herself out of her current role altogether. Her entire adult life has been spent watching after people who cannot provide for themselves; the idea that she might be the one being cared for is absurd.

To help imagine that fantasy, she had closed her eyes and controlled her breathing. Instead of allowing herself to be transported to a different outlook, however, she simply found herself thinking about her current predicament, only with her eyes shut.

In reading about the benefits of meditation, she saw it required that all thoughts must be quieted. But when she tried this, she found herself thinking about not thinking. And before long, she was thinking about how much time she had left to think about not thinking before she got back to her

Blocks. She never came close to actually quieting her mind and letting her consciousness go silent.

Such is the process of her thinking about being cared for by a paid staff of professionals. The idea comes into her mind, but almost immediately she is the caretaker again. It's an exercise in futility.

The same happens when she tries to place herself, in her current age, back in the house she grew up in as a child. This was before she and her parents moved south. She would be the only person living there. Hell, she would be the only person living in the entire country. She would wake up whenever she wanted because she would have nothing to do with her time. All day she would walk from room to noiseless room. Or sit in front of the TV watching shows she doesn't understand because the people are young and loud and no one she knew acted like that when she was their age. Music would make her restless. She would pace from window to window, looking for something to happen. Nothing ever would.

She would begin to fidget. Noises, both in her home and in the surrounding neighborhood, would make her nervous. So used to being alone, she would actually begin to dread the possibility of meeting someone else. This is partly why she would keep her blinds closed, even during the day. The other reason is that the sun would annoy her with the world it puts on display—so much life out there, even though mankind is no longer around! It's inevitable that she would long for death. Maybe even encourage it to take her from this neurotic existence.

That is what wishful thinking does to her.

Back in the gymnasium, her Blocks all around her, she realizes the people she cares for are doing more than simply giving her bodies to talk to. They keep her alive just as much as she keeps them alive. Without them, she would have nothing to do with her time. Her days would have no itinerary, no need, no urgency. She wakes with the sole focus of ensuring she can keep as many people alive and healthy as she can manage. Without them, her body would quickly get used to lying in bed all day, doing nothing.

She knows how common it is for a widower to pass away soon after their partner dies. Without someone to love, to take care of, to have as a companion, they quickly fade to nothing. Such is her case with her Blocks. If she could have picked someone else to grow old with, she would have chosen a good-looking movie star. He would tell her all about what it was like to film her favorite scenes, and she would gladly listen all day.

But instead she was given an assortment of Blocks, and she accepts this because she knows they are all she has. Without them pushing her each day, her back would give her a reason to stay in bed. Her arthritis would seem crippling. Her ankles would realize they are degenerative and refuse to let her move around all day. But because she has this need, this drive to keep her moving, keep her busy, her back remains relatively quiet, her ankles relent with minimal groans, her arthritis takes the day off.

The Blocks are keeping her alive as much as she is keeping them alive. Repeating this mantra at night, after her chores are done, even keeps the nightmares away every once in a while. Not every night, but sometimes. That is all she can ask.

42

Things have quieted since the last hurricane. She gets through her chores each day with enough time to enjoy a couple hours of sunlight. Another Block has gone to the incinerator, but this one, like the last, died of natural causes. As far as she is concerned, life is good.

As she walks from cot to cot the only noises are from the power generator and from her feet scuffling across the floor. If the power generator goes quiet during one of its cool-down cycles, if she stops walking, the entire cavernous hall will be perfectly silent.

There was a time when parades would pass by this very school, processions full of bands, dancers, floats, costumed characters. If a parade passed by right now, the marching band would be enough by itself to energize the entire gymnasium. She can't help but think of all the other ways people used to liven the city streets. Those noises made this very group home seem like a completely different place back when people were still flocking to the final settlements.

This thought leads to a memory of the lavish weddings that used to capture the entire world's attention. Nothing topped a royal wedding.

These memories can lead to nothing good; she tries to quiet the thought as soon as it enters her mind. But to no avail.

There were motorcades of limousines on their way to the cathedral. And who could forget the throngs of reporters clamoring to get the best photographs, thousands of flash bulbs going off simultaneously. People screaming with delight. A wedding gown so beautiful it looked like it was ripped from a fairy tale. One of her Blocks, a paparazzi, had even been lucky enough to document the ceremony.

Just as soon as the entire atmosphere is populated with the sights and sounds that kept her drawn to the television as a child, the princess disappears, only to be replaced in this daydream by Morgan. But surely she cannot marry the prince. The prince also disappears, and her only options are the men she actually knows. At the front of the cathedral, dressed in her gorgeous gown, she will have to pick from one of her remaining Blocks.

And when she looks at the pews, she notices that there are not hundreds of spectators there to view the proceedings. Rather, only her remaining fourteen Blocks are present. She notes with an annoyed growl that her Blocks are dispersed randomly throughout the pews in no organized fashion, and she knows this is because their cots are dispersed in the gymnasium in the same way now that there are no longer organized rows and quadrants. There are no photographers except for her Block, the paparazzi. No one else in the world is mesmerized by the footage. No one views the ceremony on TV and dreams of the same thing for their daughter one day.

There is nothing.

This is why she wishes she could have prevented her imagination from taking her there. Because now, even though she admits things are currently better than they have been any time since Elaine's death, she is sad and lonely and feeling sorry for herself. And she knows she is the only one to blame for this. That type of wedding never even appealed to her, but her mind puts her in places and scenarios that she can never control. Likewise, she has never wished to be a princess or receive the adoration of an entire country, but she likes knowing that somewhere, someone can dream of those things and hope they may come true some day.

There are no possibilities anymore other than waking up and taking care of the few remaining Blocks scattered about, or leaving them and walking to an apartment and living out her days there, which isn't really an option at all, and so no option exists.

She wonders if this fear of her circumstances, this disillusion with her place in the world, was exactly why the first men looked up at the sky and wished for something greater. Maybe life on Earth wasn't so bad, they thought, if it was only a temporary phase of their existence. Maybe being under the control of a tyrant or having an arranged marriage wasn't so bad if freedom and true love could be experienced in the afterlife. Maybe waking up each day, only to drudge through an existence of chores, all the while longing for dreams that would go unfulfilled, was tolerable because for the rest of eternity they would be reunited with lost loved ones and feel no more pain.

Was that where the very first belief in an afterlife came from, from someone unhappy with their place in the world? If that is what the belief was founded on, she thinks, the likelihood of going to heaven doesn't look very promising—things do not exist merely because you wish them to. If that were the case, a cure would have been found for the Great De-evolution.

She has herself worked into a depression that is all her own making. A good day has been tainted by daydreams and wishful thinking. But in addition to that, she has convinced herself that this world is all that exists and that her unhappiness here will not be followed by anything else, but especially not by an eternity of love and peace. Her life on this earth, for over almost an entire century, has the climax of nothing more than caring for people who would have been happier if they were never born in the first place. There is no salvation, no higher purpose.

Not only this, but she knows there cannot be a god because God would not have put her on this earth just to spend decades taking care of people who are the very cause of human extinction. No god is that spiteful.

"You're really incredible," she says aloud, to herself. None of the Blocks agree or disagree with this sentiment. "One memory of a royal wedding has you feeling sorry for yourself, has you questioning your life, badmouthing a higher power. You're a real piece of work."

But chiding herself does no good. A simple rebuke cannot counter all the self-doubt she has brought upon herself. The best thing to do, she knows, is to finish up her chores for the day and go to bed. In the morning, she may be in a better mood again. She might not only believe there is a God, but also that He has a plan for her. If she can just finish up her chores and go to sleep, everything will be better.

Maybe life is all about how you feel at the end of each day versus how you felt when you first woke up.

43

Self-pity is a disease. The shooting pain in her foot is proof of this. She didn't do anything out of the ordinary the previous day. Yes, she was tired by the time she got done cleaning and caring for the last Block, but no more tired than normal. Her back ached from bending over each cot. This is to be expected, though. Her ankles were sore from walking all day, but her foot was fine. Today, however, her foot is swollen and bruised, as if the forklift ran over it. The simple act of putting one foot in front of the other is a battle.

There is no reason for her foot to be misshapen and purple. Most people would chalk this type of injury up to "old age," that her body isn't young and healthy the way it used to be. Most people shrug it off as their body trying to tell them to take it easy and stop putting so much strain on it. Morgan doesn't feel this way, however. The only thing out of the ordinary from the day before is that she spent the time feeling sorry for herself. And today her foot feels like every bone inside must be broken.

The only explanation is quite simple: this is her body's way of identifying with the sense of defeat. In all the years she went about her chores without complaint she never woke up with random injuries. This is a punishment. But is God the one punishing her? Is the universe? Are they the same thing?

Or is she doing this to herself?

She doesn't have a reason why the pain is localized to her foot instead of, say, her elbow or wrist or neck, but she also doesn't care. The pain is a distraction to the questions that plague her. Excruciating spasms shoot up her calf and knee when she puts any weight on her foot. Luckily, one of the other caretakers was using crutches before they passed away. They are still in a locker in the corner of the gymnasium. She limps wildly toward them, stumbling repeatedly. Pulling the two wooden sticks from the metal bin, she is able to continue her rounds.

Each time she moves, though, the crutches rub away more of the tender flesh under her armpits. By the time she is done caring for the first Block, her skin is raw. She considers using one of the group home's wheelchairs to move from cot to cot, but thinks better of it. Once she gets used to the wheelchair, she won't stop using it. And once she no longer spends her days walking, her body will take the hint and begin to give up. She will be dead in a week. That is how nature works: you are only healthy until you don't think you are, and once you don't think you are, you die.

So she hobbles. Slowly.

She puts two fingers to her armpit, expecting them to come away bloody, but they are not. A blanket is wrapped around her foot to cushion it from the ground and another around the top of each crutch to pad them under her armpit.

At this pace, she will only be able to care for two Blocks each hour. Once again, she won't be done until late in the evening. A weakness comes over her, takes her strength away, as she remembers what it was like to disconnect a nutrient bag, knowing it will mean the death of someone who is counting on her.

The thought eats at her all day. She remembers the neat rows that used to line the group home. It was only a few weeks ago that Elaine died and left Morgan to care for the four quadrants of Blocks by herself. And in that short time, less than a quarter of them are still alive.

The worst part is selecting who will die next. The remaining Blocks are survivors; they struggled to live when Morgan was sick and bed-ridden. They don't deserve to persevere through that just to be picked at random for a trip to the incinerator.

Nothing positive can come from looking across the gym and picking who will have their nutrient bag disconnected next. Rather than thinking about who might be a fraction weaker than the others, she picks the very next body.

The Block, Chris, was a business continuity planner, meaning he was responsible for ensuring companies could function after any kind of crisis. People like him were in huge demand in the days following any national emergency or natural disaster. Chris didn't have a degree in the field; colleges didn't even offer degrees in something as practical as continuity of operations back when he was in school. Instead, he stumbled into the field after graduating with a degree in English—as if companies needed or wanted anyone who was an expert on William Blake's poetry. Instead, he happened into a job working with others who wrote plans and procedures for addressing every type of natural and man-made disaster and learned the field from them. For ensuring your IT systems remained available, there were disaster recovery plans. For ensuring the people who needed information had all the info they needed, there were crisis communications plans. There wasn't a single event that couldn't be planned for, even a worst case scenario, a term that people in his field were fond of using in order to get bigger budgets for their projects.

But then the Great De-evolution happened. People who were unable to care of themselves began appearing, were the only people who would ever be born again. Companies came running to Chris, asking what they should do.

All he could do was shrug. "I have absolutely no idea. I don't think this is something you can plan for."

"But that's what we pay you for."

"I'm sorry," he would tell them. "What I meant to say was, I don't think this is something we can address." And then, "This is the end."

His customers didn't like hearing the news so bluntly. They went to other professionals in the same field to see what they had to say. But the sooner they realized what Chris was saying was true, the better it would be for everyone.

And because of that, the specialized business area that was responsible for ensuring operations could continue, no matter what type of disaster struck, became one of the very first casualties of the Great De-evolution. Chris no longer had any value in the professional world, so he packed up the few things that mattered to him and began walking south.

He chose to travel on foot because his profession had taught him how unreliable roads and trains would be during emergencies. Without any place he needed to be, he took his time hiking down the Appalachian Trail, a walk he had always wanted to do anyway. Each night, he made dinner by campfires he had started himself. He watched deer walking with their young ones. He was awake for every sunrise and every sunset. Life didn't get any better. And when the trail ended, he continued south to Florida where he ended up in this home.

Morgan smiles at the man, touches his hand, then reaches over and unscrews his nutrient bag.

"Are you sure you're making the right decision?" he asks. "Have you performed a business impact analysis?"

His questions go unanswered. She would like to comfort him more, but if his death is meant to give her more time to spend caring for the living, that is what she will do. Without a word, she leaves his side and begins caring for the next Block. Chris will be dead in the morning.

44

Suddenly, she is shaking. Even before anything happens in her dream, she is filled with dread. It's the feeling she had when she was a child and knew she had earned her parents' wrath. It's the queasiness she had in middle school upon seeing a dead dog in the middle of the street. And it's the weakness that comes over her before she disconnects a Block's nutrient bag.

Brad, her soldier from quadrant 2, is standing one bed away from her. Like always, she is in her cot. It appears that he, in her place, is the one making the rounds of the facility.

Because of the Great De-evolution, Brad never had a chance to put his military training to use. He never helped occupy a foreign country, never shot his rifle at insurgents. Other than the occupation Elaine gave him, there is no reason to think he has a violent bone in his body. Even now, there is no gun in his hand, no knife at her throat. He is not torturing her. There is no hint of bodily harm, no instrument to tear her fingernails off one by one. And yet she is so scared she fears she might go to the bathroom right where she lay.

Terror makes it impossible to attempt a useless scream. Her hands remain by her side, frozen in place, unable to offer any protection. Brad looks down at her with amusement; she is not soldier material.

Her mind races, but no part of her will move. If she is paralyzed by fear, it is a fear so overwhelming that all she can do is blink. She tries to blink so hard that she wakes up, but that trick doesn't work this time. If she is motionless because she is a Block, she knows even blinking is pointless because this, too, is out of her control.

Trickles of sweat run down her forehead and, under the covers, collect on the inside of her elbows and her palms. Her clothes are soaked. Fear has a complete hold over her.

The former soldier does not interrogate or threaten her, but his mere closeness makes her want to scream. Panic is going to turn her into a raving lunatic. Maybe that is the device by which he will kill her; he won't slice her open, he will cause her to lose her mind. And because the things that happen in her dreams will occur in real life, she will wake up screaming, with no idea who she is or why she is surrounded by unmoving bodies. She will go hobbling off into the streets the exact same way George did.

Brad leans forward and inspects the body in the bed next to Morgan's. With his attention elsewhere, Morgan wishes she could sink all the way through the skinny mattress, through the floor, and into the ground.

But then the Green Beret is done looking at the body in front of him. With only a slight movement of the hips, he is now facing her. Before she can think of anything else, he moves in her direction. He is only one foot away from her now.

She is no longer breathing.

He leans over and looks directly into her pupils. If she could control one muscle right now, it would be to clench her eyes shut so she didn't have to see this man and whatever it is that he is going to do to her.

Even in her nightmare, though, she knows this is useless: *He would simply force my eyes open if he wanted them open. He is trained to get whatever he wants.*

He remains there, staring down at her. His fist doesn't smash into her nose. He doesn't wrap his fingers around her throat. But neither does he smile or offer comfort. He merely stands there, watching her without emotion, not caring about her at all.

This causes a fresh wave of fear to pulse through her. Sure, he might not torture her, but only because she is meaningless to him. His face tells her that much. She forces her eyes shut. It's better not to know how she is going to die.

She waits and waits. Nothing happens. The gym is silent.

When she opens her eyes again, he is gone. Her hand pats the mattress to make sure she can really move. She leans over and looks under her bed. He is not there. Her eyes go back across the gym. Brad is in his bed in the area that used to be quadrant 2. She looks around at her surroundings to make sure nothing has changed. Fourteen Blocks are scattered about the room. Her clothes, like in her dreams, are soaked through with sweat.

Although still unsure what any of it is supposed to mean, she finds herself thinking the Blocks aren't coming for her in these nightmares out of pure revenge, but simply because, in her dreams, she is a Block and is the next person who will have to have their nutrient bag disconnected.

It won't be anything personal, it will only be done because it is what's best for the rest of the group. That is what their unfeeling eyes tell her.

The thought is not comforting, however, because the next nightmare will surely be the last. In the first nightmares, the Blocks were all the way across the room. In this one, Brad was standing right over her. The next dream will surely start with one of her Blocks standing close enough to end it all. What should she do? Kill them all before they can get her? Never go to sleep again? Neither option is realistic.

Has everything about life always been this inevitable, or only since the Great De-evolution began? Is life measured by the amount of times you feel in control of your future and the amount of times you feel powerless?

45

Everything is more difficult on one foot. She can barely move the Blocks into new positions, and, more often than she cares to admit, leaves their bodies in the same fashion as she found them. It takes longer to get from one bed to the next. She almost breaks her neck trying to climb into the forklift so Chris's body can be taken out to the incinerator.

Halfway through her chores, she rests her head on the chest of the Block she is currently cleaning. It feels good to close her eyes and listen to the heartbeat against her ear. It's one of the most calming things she can think of.

Thump-thump, thump-thump.

Outside the gymnasium, she can hear birds calling to each other. It must be a nice time in history to be a bird, with the world almost completely returned to what it once was. With her eyes still closed, she remembers one of the nearby parks she visited with her parents when they first came to Miami. She saw more types of birds in that one place than she had seen anywhere else in her life. But as her memory takes her back to that park, she thinks of herself as she is now, an old woman walking through the sand, rather than the woman she was at the time of her visit.

She is walking in Cape Florida State Park. To the

west, separated by Biscayne Bay, sits the Miami skyline, sparkling against the sun. To the east, there is only water. She walks through sand and grass, blended together the way she has always loved. Cranes and flamingoes lift their heads just long enough to acknowledge her presence, then go back to their own routines.

McArthur, her Block who has always been undecided on what he should believe, appears next to her. Both of them went through life hearing all the things they should and shouldn't believe. Although none of it had ever sounded very convincing.

They walk together across the sand. The warm, golden grains rub between her toes. This is the first time she has seen McArthur since sending him to the incinerator. Indeed, it's the first time she has dreamed, both in her nightmares and in her daydreams, of being reunited with one of the Blocks she has euthanized.

"Beautiful place," McArthur says, seemingly not interested in exacting revenge the way her living Blocks do when they haunt her sleep.

"Yes."

Unable to control where her memory takes her, or the things her consciousness wants to focus on, she finds herself preoccupied with contemplating whether or not the park actually looks anything like this anymore. Maybe after nearly one hundred years of the Great De-evolution, it looks nothing like it had when she was younger. She likes to think, though, that this is one of the few places that has never changed, will never change, even though mankind is gone.

What does it matter how it looks in real life? she thinks. *Just enjoy the moment.*

McArthur looks over at her and smiles as if he can sense what she is thinking and agrees with the sentiment.

"I haven't been here for fifty years," she says. "I'm glad I finally get to see it again."

Even as her imagination creates wind blowing and sand that is just a little too hot, ensuring she doesn't stand in one place for too long, the obsessive part of her mind wonders if this is really what the park looked like or if her memories are making her dream into something slightly more enchanting than the park she actually visited. (If it had been this nice, why had she never returned? Why does she always think of the Grand Canyon and not this place, which happens to be so much closer?) The park is six miles off the coast of Miami, but even as recently as twenty years ago she is sure it would have been easy to find a boat able to take her that short distance.

"It's a shame more people didn't visit here," McArthur says, causing Morgan to nod in agreement.

Looking at the outline of the city in the distance, the glare of the setting sun makes it impossible to tell if they are looking at the world the way it used to be or how it is now. The sun does her a favor in this regard. It keeps her from seeing the details of each building, from seeing high-rises that might be missing their windows, from seeing apartment buildings with cracked and crumbling walls. With the sun in her eyes, it's as if the Great De-evolution has never happened. Maybe the park is not void of human life; maybe it was always this vacant and peaceful. How wonderful it is that a simple glare of light can allow someone to hope an entire city might be different than it really is. A crowded city full of every type of person, every skin color, every background, every religion. All types of music echoing through the streets. The smells of every type of food wafting through the air. The world, even in decline, had seemed so full of possibility at one time.

"Don't worry," McArthur says, noticing how her eyes refuse to veer from the nondescript outline of the buildings. "The way you remember things is much more important than how they actually end up."

"Thank you. I appreciate that."

A pelican lands near a group of flamingoes, then flies away a moment later. The sound of water crashing against the park's eastern shore is constant and soothing. A flock of white birds circles the surf.

"I'm scared," Morgan says. "I don't know what's coming next."

"No one does."

"Doesn't that scare you?"

"Whatever it is, billions of other people have already experienced it. We just happen to be the last ones."

"If you aren't scared, why am I?"

"Guilt," McArthur says, pausing to let Morgan disagree or, if she wants, change the subject completely. She remains silent and continues walking through the sand. Eventually, he adds, "There is no need for it, though. You did what you thought was best. Through everything, you handled yourself with grace. That's all you can ask of yourself. Don't blame yourself based on what others would have you believe. Guilt is a mechanism to control you, not to make you a better person."

"For someone who was supposed to have all the same questions I have, you seem to have everything figured out."

McArthur smiles. "I don't have everything figured out. I just know everything will be okay. People like you and me, we just need to see things for ourselves if we're going to understand it. There's nothing wrong with that, nothing to be ashamed of."

"I'm sorry about what happened," Morgan says, remembering back to when she disconnected his nutrient bag and left him alone to die.

The Block smiles. "Don't be sorry. You did the best you could."

"What do you think is next?"

"After this?" he says, motioning all around them at the ocean and the birds and the sand. "I have no idea. That's what makes it so exciting."

"Exciting? You're crazy."

McArthur only laughs, and Morgan finds herself thinking how amazing it is that the same person she left for dead is now amused at the things she is saying.

"Whatever it is that happens, we can't control it," McArthur says. "So why worry? No matter what, a part of me will always be with you. Just like a part of you will always be with me."

A set of fins appear in the water, and Morgan somehow knows they belong to playful dolphins rather than predatory sharks. The fins circle the water, glowing white and orange in the sun before going back under the surface and disappearing.

"I can guarantee you one thing," McArthur says. "Whatever happens next, there won't be some fiery pit or some eternal damnation. The same guys that created that concept are the same guys that want you to feel guilty all your life."

They reach the park's southern tip. From where they stand, water separates them from the rest of the world in three different directions. She can't help but wonder how many other sets of feet have stood in the exact same spot she is standing now. There was once a world full of billions of people, all trying to find their way in the world, all trying to figure out for themselves what they were supposed to be doing each day, each year, with their lives.

"Let's just enjoy the rest of our walk," McArthur says.

And he and Morgan curve along the coast until they are walking back toward the direction they came from.

She opens her eyes. Her head is still resting on the Block's chest. The heartbeat is still soothing in its steady pattering.

Thump-thump, thump-thump.

Back to her chores.

46

Her foot is just as swollen and purple as it was the day before. Her eyes close, allowing her to remember her dream and how nice the sand felt on her bare feet, how she had been able to walk without shooting pains. Another day on the crutches will do her no good, but does what she has to do.

Neither the scuffing of her feet nor the thud of her crutches can be heard over the howl of the wind and rain. Water is trickling in through one of the windows where the seal has deteriorated.

Oh well, she thinks. *Luck doesn't last an entire lifetime.*

A towel collects the drops as they fall, but it is only a temporary solution. Soon, the thick cotton is completely saturated and a puddle spreads out across the floor.

None of her Blocks are concerned about the hurricane. If they aren't worried, she tells herself, she should try not to be either.

Although another Block is gone, she still has no chance of getting to everyone in one day. Her foot ensures that much.

What's next? If I'm not sick, my foot hurts. And the Blocks are the ones who always pay the price. Unless I die first, this is just going to keep happening until I can't even take care of one person.

She finds herself at the bed of Tori, her famous chef.

Tori used the Great De-evolution to her advantage the way all great artists found inspiration from hard times. As other people were closing their restaurants, Tori decided it was the perfect time to finally open the restaurant of her dreams. With farms going out of business, with grocery stores and butcher shops closing their doors, Tori turned to the food processor for salvation.

Her restaurant used the same model of food processor that everyone else was provided with, but Tori turned the generated meals into works of art. The same way a trash collector recreated a Picasso with random junk, Tori used the food processor to recreate famous meals that used to be found in five-star restaurants around the world. She didn't just present a plate of Maine Lobster with butter, she took the time to make the same citrus butter sauce that Chef Pietro had used for so many years. She didn't just present her customer with glazed chicken, she took the time to make each individual ingredient needed to bake the chicken in a sweet champagne glaze, the same way Chef DeAngelo made famous.

The restaurant didn't turn a profit. In fact, most of her customers didn't even pay for their meals. This was back when currencies around the world were almost worthless, so receiving money wouldn't have made much of a difference. But that didn't matter to her. She hadn't opened the restaurant to become rich, she opened it because it had always been her dream and she wanted to achieve it before it was too late.

Tori says, "It wasn't the famous Parisian café I dreamed of as a kid, but it was enough."

"I wish you would have taught me some of your tricks. I've gone through every standard recipe the food processor can make."

"I would have liked that."

Morgan begins to say something else, but a great howl of wind makes her shudder. A second puddle is forming, this one on the other side of the gym from where the soaked towel is no longer controlling the first leak. Where are the buckets? She cannot remember the last caretaker that needed a bucket or what they might have done with them. There is no time to investigate; she has to keep moving.

She looks down at her content chef, takes comfort in knowing the woman lived the life she had always wanted, then reaches over and disconnects the nutrient bag keeping her alive.

The thought re-enters her mind: *How long can this keep going on? This is just going to keep happening until I can't even take care of one person.*

In the morning, if there is still a roof over them, if they aren't flooded out altogether, she will take Tori's body out to the incinerator.

47

When Morgan opens her eyes, Erin has already crossed most of the room. She is only three feet away from where Morgan is lying in bed. The marathon runner used to jog through miles of land during her races. Now, her feet shuffle the same way Morgan's do when she is caring for each Block. Soon, she will be at Morgan's side.

Erin's feet bring her another foot closer.

There is no telling what she will do. Her eyes, like all the rest, are emotionless. They are eyes capable of anything.

Now, she is only one foot away.

This is only a dream. This is only a dream. The thought does not slow Morgan's soaring heart rate.

In her mind, Morgan is screaming for help, she is pleading not to be hurt. She is asking for forgiveness. But in the reality of her dream, she is doing none of this. Her body is still. She doesn't get to plead her case. Tears pour from the corners of her eyes, the only response of any kind she is capable of offering.

Erin is here now, standing over her. Their eyes meet. There is no more time for begging or prayer. There is no more time for regret or self-pity.

The runner's eyes are still void of any emotion. There is no telling what Erin has planned.

Please, just make it quick.

But Erin doesn't reach for Morgan's throat. She doesn't produce a knife from behind her back. She lowers herself until she is sitting on the edge of Morgan's bed.

I did my best. I did what I thought was right for everyone.

Erin looks around the room, then back at Morgan. The gym is perfectly quiet.

I'm suffering as much as you. You don't know what it's been like. I know I was responsible for caring for all of you, and I know I failed. But I did my best. I swear, I did.

"Quiet," Erin says, even though Morgan has not actually said anything.

Morgan's eyes stop darting around the room. Her heart skips a beat. She wonders if Erin really said something or if she imagined it the way she imagined the other Blocks' threats and, really, the way she has imagined their entire lives. If she could just close her eyes and make all of this go away she would.

Erin is still sitting on her bed, but now, instead of looking down at Morgan, she is looking around at the expanse of the mostly empty gymnasium. At various times during its existence, the room has held screaming and laughing kids, each having all the fun a child could ever hope for. It has held hundreds of retired teachers and other out-of-work professionals, no longer needed once the world started changing, all working toward one goal. And it held all the Blocks who were abandoned by their families as mankind faded away.

This is what Erin seems to be thinking about when she says, "There are only a few of us left."

Morgan looks at Erin's lips. She is sure these words were really spoken. These actually are Erin's words, not the things Morgan might have imagined. In the confines of her sleep, there may be no difference between what Erin says and what she might have said—both are created by Morgan's brain and delivered by her subconscious—but the difference is distinct in her dream.

Please, Morgan thinks, wishing she could force her lips to move. *Please don't hurt me. I did my best.*

She is crying again. A steady trickle of tears is running down her cheeks.

"Quiet," Erin says again. "I know you did your best."

Then why are you doing this to me?

"What am I doing to you?" Erin says.

The runner stops looking at the few remaining cots spread out across the otherwise empty floor and turns once again to look down at Morgan.

"Yes, I hear you," Erin says, although Morgan still has not said anything.

Then you have to know I didn't want anyone to die. I didn't want anyone to suffer.

"I know that. Of course I know that."

Then why are you doing this to me? Why do you want to hurt me?

"I don't want to hurt you."

Erin puts her hand on Morgan's shoulder. But instead of holding Morgan in place while the attack commences—as if Morgan could move if she wanted to—the hand rests there, gently.

Morgan is crying harder now. Her chest heaves with the force of her sobs, her throat gurgles, her eyes close. Without even thinking, she wipes the snot away from her nose.

She can move.

Through it all, Erin's hand remains delicately on Morgan's shoulder. The runner's eyes are still without emotion, but what Morgan once saw as cold hatred seems more like a sense of acceptance with the world and with everything that must happen in it.

Morgan wipes another batch of tears away from her eyes. When she can see clearly again, she notices Erin is sitting there as if there is nothing to be sad about, or happy or afraid or anxious or anything else; there are only the things you allow to have power over you, and if you don't allow them to affect you, they aren't really there at all.

A new round of sobs comes over Morgan. She is not crying because she is afraid, though. She is not crying because she feels vindicated. She cries because of everything she has ever done in her life—the good parts, the bad parts, the things she wishes she could do all over again. All of it.

When the crying subsides, she says, "We're almost at the end, aren't we?"

"Yes," Erin says. "But that's not a reason to be upset."

Erin has spoken with a wisdom Morgan has never attributed to her before. She was always the Block who had liked to run outdoors and now was confined to an over-sized room. She wishes she could have had at least one real conversation with each of the people around her before she started creating fictitious lives and personalities to each of them.

Erin smiles. Maybe she is thinking the same thing.

But then Morgan's thoughts take a darker turn again. She thinks about how many Blocks she has killed in the past weeks, about how killing just one was enough for some people to say she would be spending eternity in hell. She thinks about whether or not she will see her parents again, see her friends again, or if everyone simply ceases to exist. How could you not be afraid of the end with all those possibilities?

"Listen," Erin says, patting Morgan's arm, "I can guarantee you that whatever is next, it won't be like anything you've been taught. How would those people know what's next if they haven't been there yet?"

"But what if there isn't anything at all?"

"If there is nothing, there is nothing to worry about."

"What do you think happens when we die?"

"I have no idea. No one knows for sure. Anyone that thinks they know is probably wrong."

"How can you be so calm about all of this?"

"What's the point in worrying? We have all lived the life we had to live. What else is there? I can promise you one thing, though."

"What's that?"

"I'll always be a part of you. All of us"—she motions around the room at the few remaining cots, but also where all the other beds once were—"will be with you. And you'll always be with us. Maybe we won't have another life, maybe we won't have some kind of conscious afterlife in the clouds, but that doesn't change what actually happened here. It doesn't change that you did your best with the life you had. Maybe we won't all be gathered in heaven. Maybe we won't all be reincarnated as birds. But somewhere, somehow, the memory of you caring for us, all the times we've shared, of the people you loved before you arrived here, all of it will live on. Maybe it will only live on in diaries or in pictures, but maybe the essence of what you did here, of one person trying to care for everyone as much as she knew how, maybe that will live on forever in another form."

"Do you really believe that?"

"Anything is possible. It's also possible that we'll all be flying across the Atlantic Ocean looking for a place to lay our eggs, and I'll look over at one of the other birds in the flock and know that I've seen her somewhere before, and that she was special to me then, just as she is special to me now."

"I'm scared."

"I know, but you don't have to be. I'm here. We're all here."

There is always the same amount of energy in the universe. One form of energy gives way to another, but always in the same amounts. Science has proven this. What this means is that somewhere out there, the energy of her parents, her old friends, the Blocks she has had to sacrifice and also the ones who died of natural causes, are all out there. And hers will be there as well, soon. Maybe in the form of souls. Maybe something else.

In this life, the Blocks were trapped in the shells of bodies that were incapable of moving or talking. In their next existence, though, whatever it is, their energy will be just like everyone else's. This is what she has come to believe.

Of the things she does not know, she is not afraid. It could be terrifying to think that she is utterly alone, the very last person in the world. There are millions of acres of abandoned lands, empty forests, cemeteries. There are final settlements similar to hers where the people have already passed away without anyone to bury them. But she doesn't worry about any of this because she knows everything she has seen, everyone she has loved, is still out there somewhere, in some form. Maybe just a memory, but also, maybe something greater.

She doesn't know what will be next. It no longer matters. Maybe life doesn't start the first time you smile and end the last time something makes you happy. Maybe it isn't defined by the first and last time you believe in something greater than yourself. Maybe life isn't measured in heartbeats or curiosity or even in acts of love.

Maybe life is whatever you make of it.

"What happens now?" she asks.

"The dream ends."

ACKNOLWEDGEMENTS

I am once again indebted to many people for their support: as always, Jodie McFadden, for her constant encouragement and optimism; Derek Prior, for a great edit of the manuscript; Bruce Clark and Anna Stewart for their wonderful comments and suggestions on the story; and everyone at Authors On The Air, GoodReads, and in the BJJ and MMA communities who read my other novels and recommended them to their friends. Without their support, I would be no where.

Want to receive updates on my future books and get some great freebies? Sign up for my newsletter at: http://chrisdietzel.com/mailing_list/

ABOUT THE AUTHOR

Chris graduated from Western Maryland College (McDaniel College). His dream is to write the same kind of stories that have inspired him over the years.

His others novels have become Amazon Best Sellers, been featured on Authors on the Air, and were voted as some of GoodReads top 10 "Most Interesting Books" the year they were published.

CPSIA information can be obtained
at www.ICGtesting.com
Printed in the USA
BVHW031821300721
613289BV00012B/88